Samantha's Life
Part II

Samantha's Life Part II

Betsy Baker Dietz

iUniverse, Inc.
Bloomington

Samantha's Life Part II

iUniverse books may be ordered through booksellers or by contacting:

iUniverse
1663 Liberty Drive
Bloomington, IN 47403
www.iuniverse.com
1-800-Authors (1-800-288-4677)

ISBN: 978-1-4759-6612-1 (sc)
ISBN: 978-1-4759-6614-5 (ebk)

Library of Congress Control Number: 2012923076

Printed in the United States of America

iUniverse rev. date: 12/05/2012

Chapter 1

Settling In

My dad parked his Tahoe behind Baylor Hall and helped me lug my stuff up to the second floor. When we met Dawn and Cindy on the stairwell, they eyed my good-looking dad. They started laughing, and that made me giggle, too. "What was that all about?" Dad asked.

"They find you attractive," I said. I glanced at him and saw a slight smile come to his lips, so I didn't explain how I'd tried to deflect their attraction to him all last year with comedic remarks.

This year, Nancy and I were in Room 201, in a much nicer dorm than the freshman dorm we'd been in last year. When we got to the room, I opened the window and was pleased to find that the large oak tree outside gave us some shade from the afternoon sun without obliterating our view of the quad. The quad was a huge, grassy expanse closed in by red-brick buildings.

One more load and we had all my stuff in my room. Dad gave me a quick kiss on the cheek, and we said good-bye to one another. He was leaving when Nancy came in. "Well, here we are again," I said to Nancy when he was gone.

"For better or for worse," she replied.

"I'm really going to study hard this year." I plopped my suitcase onto my choice of the twin beds, smiling inwardly because I thought mine had the better mattress.

"Like you did last year? Yeah, right." She started shoving things into her dresser drawers, and she muttered, "I hope this wasn't a mistake."

"What? Bringing too many gigantic bras?"

She sighed and pushed a strand of black hair behind her ear. "Even my own roommate can't ignore the size of my breasts," she muttered. Her hair had grown to medium length, and it still had a hint of the burgundy color we'd experimented with in June. She'd tried to color over it, but when the light hit it a certain way, I could still see it.

A lot had happened to us over the summer of 1999. I had lost my virginity, and she and a guy named Todd had broken up in July. Nancy hadn't been prepared for that and had almost decided not to come back to Fermen because of it, but I convinced her we'd have a great time. I hadn't paid that much attention to their romance last year. I mean, I'd known she went out with him from time to time, but she'd never really talked about him much, and now she was acting as if it were the end of the world. She was still worried about the emotional ordeal of seeing Todd on campus. "Just flip him the bird," I had said, and that had made her smile. Now that I thought about it, I guessed it would be hard for her to face an unwanted breakup. Maybe she'd gotten the idea that with tits like hers she could have any guy she wanted. Or maybe *I*'d just thought I could have any guy I wanted if I had large breasts, which I didn't.

We had decorated our room in black, white, and red: black curtains to keep the morning sun out of our faces when we wanted to sleep in, white bedspreads, and red lamps and candleholders. Someone had given Nancy a black-and-white zebra-striped rug, and it covered most of our bedroom floor. We had our own bathroom and no suitemates, which was much better than the arrangement we'd had in the freshman dorms. Our place was like a tiny apartment. A short hallway connected a small study room to our bedroom, and the bath was off the hallway. We got a telephone a day later. Our room was perfect, then.

Nancy's cousin, Marsha, and Marsha's roommate, Tina, who lived down the hall, popped in after we'd gotten settled. "Nice!" Marsha exclaimed. "My room looks like we gathered whatever we could find at the Goodwill store to decorate—well, actually, that's what we did. Nothing matches."

"Ours is *shabby chic*," Tina offered, and we all laughed. Unlike her name, Tina was tall and birdlike, and she moved her hands extravagantly, which made almost anything she said seem funny.

"Better than prison décor," Marsha said. I nodded, but I was noting the difference in Nancy's bust and Marsha's. Nancy's cousin apparently hadn't inherited the big-boob gene. "Let's all have dinner together," Marsha suggested.

"I can't go out right now. I'm busted," I said.

"I only meant the cafeteria."

"Oh, okay." So we all headed over to see what was on the menu. It turned out we had a choice of roasted turkey or Salisbury steak, mashed potatoes, green beans, roasted mixed veggies, and rolls. There was also the usual soup and salad bar and an option of a sandwich and fries. I opted for the salad bar. As I was piling lettuce onto my plate, I felt Nancy grab my arm. "Isn't that Wanda at that table by the window?" she asked.

I looked, and sure enough, it was. "What is she doing here?" I hissed. "She was supposedly suspended."

"Maybe she's just visiting someone," Nancy whispered.

I almost lost my appetite, but decided that Tina and Marsha would wonder what was going on if I didn't eat, and it wouldn't help anything, anyway. Nancy and I headed for a table across the room from Wanda, and Tina and Marsha followed.

"Who are you talking about?" Marsha demanded, and Nancy quickly pointed Wanda out to her.

"That's the girl who nearly ruined my whole college career and maybe my life," I said. "It's a long story. Here's the gist: she lied and said I bought beer for minors last semester, when it was her own boyfriend who did it. She had two girls swear to her story, and if one of them hadn't finally told the truth, I'd have been suspended and lost my scholarship."

Tina, who was listening intently, flung her hands to her sides and said, "What an evil bitch!" Her hand knocked a salt shaker off the table, and she looked so funny in her motions that it broke the tension, and we all nearly laughed ourselves into hysterics. I glanced over at Wanda again and found her staring in our direction.

Later that night, Nancy and I decided Wanda's presence had to be a fluke. "I wish she had been ordered not to set foot on campus," I groused. "It's not like I ever wanted to see her face again."

"Relax," Nancy said. "It's probably eating her alive that she can't take classes here this semester. If you see her again, wait until she has some people around her, and then ask if she was able to get into a community college or if she's working at McDonald's instead."

I giggled at the thought of lovely Wanda flipping burgers or standing behind a cash register in a McDonald's uniform.

"Forget her. We need to think about us," Nancy said, settling back on her pillows. "This is our year to shine. Let's get some sleep."

Nancy and I figured we'd probably spend almost all our time together, because neither of us was dating anyone, and we didn't really want to be dating. I felt optimistic about the upcoming year. Just as I was about to drift off to sleep, Nancy tossed out an interesting idea. "We should go to the health department clinic in Roanoke and get some birth control pills," she murmured, as though half-asleep.

"Why? We're not dating, and we don't want to be dating, remember?"

"Even so, who knows when she might meet a guy and want to get laid?" Nancy asked, and I could swear she was snoring softly before she even finished the sentence. I lay there and considered what she'd said. She had to be joking. I was almost 100 percent sure she was still a virgin.

Chapter 2

A Wild Feeling Inside

Four days after we arrived on campus, our Gamma Nu sorority had its first meeting of the year, so we headed off to the sorority house. The scene was much different from last year's "truth" ceremony when we had been formally brought in as members—no laundry-room bit with white sheets over the washer and dryer to create a "tabernacle of truth" this time. Fifteen girls were present. We sat on the lumpy green sofa and in various chairs scattered in the front room. Since our old president had graduated, Danna, the current vice president, brought up the issue of Gamma Nu's yearly Christmas project for the local shelter for abused women. She had asked permission for the sorority to sell popcorn at Fermen's weekly movie night event. She said her father had agreed to provide a large popcorn maker for us to use, one he'd used from time to time at his car dealership. The big bonus for us was that, once we signed to be the popcorn vendors, no other groups would be allowed to sell popcorn at the movie nights. The first movie night was in three days, so we had to act right away. We quickly voted to approve that plan, and Danna said she would go over and sign us on as vendors that same day. Nancy and I volunteered to help set up the vending space and sell the popcorn each week, while Danna agreed to serve as a backup or to help us find others to fill in if we were unable to do that on any given week.

Next Danna announced that we would elect new officers. "Who's willing to serve?" she asked. Nancy and I both raised our hands. Clarissa, a redhead, and Jane, a feisty blonde, also raised their hands. Danna gave quick review of the responsibilities for each job, along with her recommendations on which of us would fit best each position. Danna made a motion, and a girl named Christy seconded it, so Danna called for a quick show of hands in favor. I was elected vice president, and Nancy was elected treasurer. Clarissa, a former council member, became president, and Jane became the new secretary. The vote was unanimous. *This is just bullshit,* I thought. Then Danna asked the newly elected leaders to meet with her for a few minutes afterward, when she would transfer the journals from the previous officers to us and answer any questions we might have. *At least it has a bit of substance*, I had to admit. We had no further business but pigging out on wine and cheese, so Danna announced that our next meeting would be on September 21.

I looked at the other girls, the ones who weren't officers, and wondered why they hadn't wanted to volunteer. I guessed it was enough for them simply to belong to a sorority. *It's still a good organization*, I told myself, but I grew more and more irritated, without knowing why. *We do a lot of nice work in the community.*

My pompom squad practice was set to start the next week. I wondered if new pompom leaders would be elected. Tammy had been a good leader, but she and her coleader,

Hillary, fought a lot. I decided I might go for it if I had a chance to become a squad leader. It would look good on a resume later. *Would that be taking on too much?* I didn't think so.

When we got back to the dorm, I told Nancy I wished I could make this a brand-new year with all new friends, except for her, of course. But that was impossible if I stayed in Gamma Nu and on the pompom squad. I had suddenly developed a wild feeling inside, and most of the people around me just made me want to scream. Our sorority sisters suddenly looked like carbon copies of one another. When I mentioned it, Nancy said she felt the same way. "Did you notice how there was no discussion over the election, no real competition, just a show of hands? They're so much alike we might as well belong to flock of sheep as a sorority," I said. "I'm going to just shut them out, for the most part."

All that week, I was trying to be the perfect student, keeping my resolution to study more and my other resolution to make my dad proud. I had decided to get an associate in science degree at Fermen instead of going for the associate in arts, as most of my sorority sisters were. I felt that having a good base of science and math would keep me flexible, since at this point, I still had no idea of what I wanted to do with my life. I was lucky to be attending this private two-year college in the first place, especially since I'd come dangerously close to being thrown out last year (through no fault of my own). It seemed that I needed to redefine my goals, if not to change them, to reinforce my desire to achieve them. The more I thought about this, the clearer my goals became: One, to not only do well academically but to do enough community service projects to beef up my resume; two, to make dad very proud; and three, to find a boyfriend who wasn't crazy, someone stable, someone I could depend on. The more I thought about it, the more logical it seemed to keep the priorities of those goals in that order. I didn't see how I could go wrong if I did that.

On Friday night, Nancy and I popped corn to sell at Fermen's movie night for the sorority. They showed a cheesy old horror film, *Night of the Living Dead*, on a huge screen set up in the quad. The movie didn't disturb me as much as the laughter that rang out in the quad when someone was killed or when the zombies ate their victims. *This whole crowd is sick*, I thought. We raised a hundred and three dollars that night, which went into our project fund to buy Christmas gifts for the women at the shelter. Nancy, who also found the movie amusing, said, "I guess there's nothing like the smell of buttered popcorn and the sight of zombies chowing down to whet the appetite."

On Saturday, we went to the Delta Pi Lambda fraternity's dance. The fraternity was across the road from the main campus in a run-down, three-story house that looked as if it had been built in the early 1900s. It was hard to tell much about the inside because the lights were so low. I wondered if we'd see that the place was filthy if they turned more lights on. There were several kegs of beer in the corner of the large front room, and a band called Red Dawg was playing in the back of the room. I'd never heard of them, but they weren't that bad. They did oldies and covers of current pop songs. I saw Doug, a guy I had met exactly a year ago at this same dance. I asked if he remembered meeting me, and he said, "I remember" and walked off. I was furious at his rudeness, so I asked some stupid guy named Evan to dance with me.

Evan couldn't dance, but he tried because he thought I liked him. It was embarrassing to be seen with him flailing around, so I got rid of him after a dance or two. I didn't want him to become too attached to me.

Later, a cute guy named David Martin asked me to dance, and we got along well. David was tall, with dark hair, and he had soulful, dark eyes. He even smelled good. I asked what he was wearing, and he said it was Grey Flannel aftershave.

"Can I get you a drink?" he asked after two dances.

I realized he was looking back toward those kegs, so I quickly said, "Yes, but not that. I don't do alcohol, ever."

When I said that he smiled and said, "Neither do I. I could now, I guess, but avoiding it has become so ingrained in me that I never do. My dad is a preacher."

"I don't drink because my mother was killed by a drunk driver."

I thought he was about to give me the standard "I'm sorry to hear that" line, but he just looked at me for a moment and said, "I don't know what to say." Then he seemed to remember how the conversation had started and said, "I think they have some sodas in the kitchen." As soon as he left the room, Nancy came over and said, "Nice going. He's really good-looking, and mine's not so bad, either." She nodded in the direction of a stocky guy with brown hair who waved. "That's Rob," she said before heading back to him.

David came back with two cold bottles of Coke, and we stepped out onto the front porch of the frat house. "So, how did you come to join Delta Pi Lambda?" I asked.

"Maybe just to irritate the folks back home," he said. "Who knows?" We heard the lead singer announce that the band was taking a break, and the noise level inside suddenly went down dramatically. More people came out onto the porch, so I didn't hesitate when David took my hand and started walking toward the backyard. There was an open, grassy area with trees on either side.

We stood in the shadow of the trees a bit awkwardly, until I looked up and saw a lovely rounded moon. "Should I be careful of werewolves tonight?" I asked.

"Well, the full moon was actually a couple of days ago, but sometimes its effects can be retroactive." He leaned down and nipped at my throat, and I felt it all the way to my toenails. When I didn't resist, he stopped and kissed my mouth, then moved back to my neck. When I was thoroughly turned on, we heard the band tuning up inside. He said, "Come on, there's a song for a night like this."

When we got inside, he spoke to the lead singer, pulled out his wallet, and gave him some cash. Within seconds, they opened their set with Firefall's, "You Are the Woman," and David pulled me onto the dance floor. I felt like a princess for probably the first time in my life. David made me feel as if I really was the woman of his dreams, someone he'd seen and fallen for in an instant, and I felt the same way about him. *How can I be so lucky?* I wondered. We stayed there dancing and talking until the band stopped playing, and it felt like we'd always been together; it was kind of surreal. When he walked me back to my dorm, there were no more werewolf kisses. He simply said good night and kissed my lips gently.

Nancy was sleeping when I got in, so I was torn between waking her to tell her about this miracle of meeting David and holding it all inside for a while. I opted to lie in bed reliving my perfect evening and thanking my lucky stars.

Chapter 3

A Mixed Basket

The next morning, I started telling Nancy about my time with David in excruciating detail. When I got to the part about him paying the band to play "You Are the Woman," she rolled her eyes and said, "And then he took you upstairs and screwed you, right?"

"No! Then he kept dancing and talking with me until the band packed up. Then he walked me home, and then he gave me a light kiss on the lips." I looked at her and asked, "What's wrong? Are you jealous?"

Nancy scratched her nose and said, "To me, it just sounds like he's trying to get in your pants."

I couldn't understand why she wasn't happy for me. *Didn't I practically cut flips in June when she was so elated over being with Todd?* I just looked at her and asked, "Did someone piss on your cornflakes?"

Her lower lip started to quiver, and she said, "I ran into Todd last night. He was in a bar on Main Street, practically crawling all over some redhead." Nancy threw her hands over her face and started sobbing.

I put my hand on her shoulder and waited until she'd let most of the emotion out. When the worst of it was over, I said, "That asshole isn't worth that many tears," and she started laughing and crying at the same time. "Does he know you saw him?" I asked.

"I don't think so."

I walked over to the window and looked out over the quad, thinking and willing some face to come to mind, some guy I could hook Nancy up with that wouldn't be a turd. "We'll have to work on this," I said.

It was nearly lunchtime when someone knocked on our door. I jumped to open it, hoping it was David. A middle-aged man stood in the hallway. "Are you Samantha Fredrich?" he asked.

"Yes."

"Then these are for you," he said, pushing a basket of mixed pink-and-purple flowers into my hands. He was gone before I had time to react. I took them inside and opened the card with trembling hands. It read, "You *are* the woman. Thanks for a lovely evening. I'm really busy this week, but I can't wait to see you again. David."

Even Nancy was impressed. I took off in search of Marsha, borrowed her digital camera, and took pictures of my floral arrangement.

On Monday, I had a political science class and was stunned to see Wanda in a seat near the front row. I nudged Danna, from Gamma Nu, who was beside me, and whispered, "What's she doing here? Last semester, Fritz told me she'd been kicked out."

Danna held up one finger, as if telling me to wait a minute. Then she scribbled something into a composition book and handed it to me. Her note read, "Her dad gave big money to the building fund, so the dean changed his mind. She's on probation instead, but she's still off the cheerleading squad."

I felt my face grow hot as my pulse sped up. I was so angry my hands started shaking. I wanted to go up front and shake Wanda out of her seat. Instead, I wrote, "Screw the dean!" and underlined it twice.

Danna wrote back, "She may have done that, too."

I was steaming. I didn't hear a thing the professor said that day. I did have the presence of mind to take a class syllabus so I'd have the reading assignments.

After class, I headed off to pompom squad's first meeting in the women's locker room at the gymnasium. Tammy called the meeting to order and brought up the election of leaders. She said she'd like to serve again and asked who else would be interested. I raised my hand and noticed that Hillary did not. Tammy cleared her throat and said, "Well, this ought to be interesting. I have one other item of new business. We have another candidate for coleader as well, but I told her to wait and give us a few minutes to present her candidacy before she came in today, because she's a former cheerleader, not someone who has been on our squad. However, she's fully qualified." Just then, Wanda walked into the locker room.

I wanted to scream, but a memory of my mother kept me from it. I'd heard about Mom's accident and gotten to the hospital in time to see her before she died. One side of her face was badly bruised and swollen as she lay on a gurney in the ER under a thin white blanket. They had done CAT scans and found extensive internal bleeding. I was surprised she was even conscious, but when she heard

I was there, she demanded to see me before they took her for surgery. She grabbed my hand and said, "Don't hate your grandfather." She was struggling to breathe, but she clutched my hand and added, "Don't let bitterness poison your life." She knew who had crashed into her car that evening and had even guessed why. She whispered, "If you want to hate something, hate alcohol."

I believe she hung onto her life with all her might as long as she could just so she could tell me that. She didn't make it through her surgery. As I thought about that evening, I felt my mother's strength of character rush into me, calming me.

Tammy looked at me. "Would you feel comfortable serving as coleader with Wanda, if she's elected?" she asked. At the same time, I felt Wanda's eyes on me and glanced up at her.

"Of course," I said.

Slips of paper were passed around. "Okay, write two names, and only two, on the ballots," Tammy said.

Hillary was enlisted to collect the ballots and call out the votes. She wrote our names on an erasable board and put hash marks under our names to make the tally. Wanda got only five votes, so Tammy and I were elected coleaders of the squad. I'm not really sure I could have stayed on the squad if it had been me and Wanda, but I felt proud that I had taken the high road.

After the meeting, Wanda cornered me and said, "You hate me, don't you?"

I didn't answer, but I stared at her.

"Why can't you just get over it?" she asked. Incredibly, it sounded like a sincere question.

"You don't have any idea what your lies might have done to me, do you?" I asked. She just stood there looking at me, so I said, "I don't have a rich father who can come in and fix everything if I screw up. I'm only able to be here because I earned a scholarship based on academic merit. If your plan had worked out, I would have lost that scholarship, and my whole chance at going to college would be down the toilet! All because of your fucking lies! And to answer your question: no, I don't hate you, but I sure don't like you."

Wanda bit her lip, and I saw tears in her eyes. "I'm sorry," she said, and she started to walk away, but she turned and said, "You're bigger than me" before she left the locker room. I slammed my fist against the wall and hurt my knuckles. I had wanted to slam it into her gut when she cornered me. I knew that she couldn't be sincere in her apology. Girls like Wanda just did whatever they felt they had to do to get whatever they wanted. I stopped and thought about it for a minute, but I couldn't figure out what she had wanted in this case. *Why did she turn on the tears? It doesn't matter—whatever she wants, she isn't going to get it,* I thought. *I'll throw her off pompom squad the first time she messes up, and I won't have to wait long. She'll show up late or drunk or both before long.* I walked out of the locker room with a smile on my face.

I kept thinking about David and looking for him around campus, but I didn't see him until he found me in the library on Friday morning. I thanked him for the flowers and invited him to come and see them because they were still pretty. I'd been changing their water every day and trimming their stems every other day to make them last. "How'd you like to go with me to O'Grady's for dinner?" he asked me.

My heart skipped a beat because I knew O'Grady's was an expensive place. I was tempted to ditch my obligation for the evening, but that wouldn't look good, since I was vice president of Gamma Nu. I bit my lip and said, "I'd love to, but could we go tomorrow night instead? I'm supposed to sell movie night popcorn for Gamma Nu tonight."

"Sure, Saturday's fine."

"Want to join me in the quad tonight?"

"I'd like to, but I can't," he said. "I only allow myself one night a week to go out, because I'm hoping to transfer into the premed program at Washington and Lee when I finish here. It's very demanding, and I know competition will be stiff."

"Do you go to O'Grady's a lot?" I asked.

"No, I've never been, but I'd like to try it, especially with you—hey, do you smell something burning?" he asked, looking around as if suddenly concerned about our safety.

I sniffed the air. "No. I can't smell anything. If there were smoke, wouldn't it trip the fire alarm?"

David relaxed and said, "It must be the money that's burning a hole in my pocket."

I punched his shoulder and said, "Goofball."

Chapter 4

The Royal Treatment

O'Grady's was elegant, as I'd imagined it would be. Everything was bathed in a soft glow from the crystal chandeliers overhead. The dishes were mauve and embossed with a floral design. Cut-crystal glasses sparkled on the tables. David had reserved a table in a quiet corner. When the server came, he was wearing a pleated white shirt, a cummerbund, and a black bow tie. He handed us menus that opened into about six pages and lit a little oil lamp in the center of our table. Before asking for our drink orders, he offered us samples of several house wines, but we refused, of course. "I'll just have water," I said. David ordered iced tea. I couldn't believe the extensive selection on the menu. For dinner, David ordered prime rib, asparagus tips, and a twice-baked potato. I felt confused by the number of choices, so I just ordered the exact same thing.

"Would you like an appetizer?" the server asked. David looked up at me, and I shook my head.

"No, thank you," David said. "We're saving room for dessert." I smiled at him. When the server left, David asked,

"Like it?" His eyes were merry, so I knew he could tell that I did.

I reached across the table and squeezed his hand. "This is the most elegant place I've ever seen."

Over dinner, he told me more about his father, who was pastor of a popular nondenominational church in Martinsville, Virginia. Like me, David had lost his mother a few years ago. His mother had died of breast cancer. However, we didn't linger on sad topics for very long.

I told him about Nancy, and he asked, "Is she that girl with the huge breasts?" I studied his face to see if he was interested in her, but he said, "A fluke of nature. My roommate, Houston, is too, but in a different way. He acts like he belongs to the 1960s era and describes himself as 'a hippy freak.'"

"Does he wear tie-dyed shirts and flash the peace sign?" I asked.

"No, but he sits in our room smoking pot and staring out the window a lot. When he's not doing that, he's in a corner strumming his guitar."

I giggled and asked, "What about your other friends?"

David shrugged. "I don't really have time for friends, but I guess my friends are the other premed hopefuls. They're the ones I see on a regular basis in classes. We get along, except for this one guy named Steve Corson, who seems to dislike me for no reason." David shifted his weight and leaned forward in his chair. "Have you ever known anyone like that?"

I spent the next few minutes telling him about my experience with Wanda.

We were stuffed by the time we finished dinner, but David wanted to keep his promise about dessert, so we decided to split a slice of cheesecake. Before we left, David asked me to go with him to the homecoming dance that was coming up in three weeks. I was elated.

Back at my dorm, I got a few more of those "werewolf kisses" he'd given the night I met him, but that was it. I offered to bring him up to my room, but he said he'd better not. "See you next Saturday?" he asked, and I nodded. "It might be a fast-food joint next time," he warned.

"I don't care if it's the college cafeteria," I said. By the time he left, I was sure I was in love.

I wanted to talk to Nancy, but when I went into our room, I saw she had Rob in bed with her. They hadn't bothered to turn out the lights. *Well, great! Maybe she'll stop pining over Todd,* I thought. I grabbed my blankets and pillow and slept in our study room in Nancy's canvas chair, which unfolds into a recliner. I didn't mind, because I was dreaming about the times she'd be sleeping in the chair while I had David in our room. I went to sleep trying to picture the perfect dress for the homecoming dance.

Chapter 5

The Perfect Dress

The next weekend, Nancy and I gave Tina some gas money to take us into Roanoke to shop for dresses for the homecoming dance. Tina planned to attend the dance with a guy name Perry, so she wanted to look at dresses, too. She would have let us ride along for nothing, but we thought paying for the gas was the right thing to do. Rob had invited Nancy to go to the dance with him, and his presence in her life had really brightened her countenance. I mused that it was amazing the changes one week could bring in a girl's life.

None of us had a lot of money, but we'd heard they were having a sale at J.C. Penney, so we decided to check it out. I had a hundred dollars, because my grandfather on Dad's side of the family had sent it as an early Christmas gift when he heard I needed a formal dress. I wanted a jewel-tone dress because I figured it could double as a Christmas dress. Besides, my mother had always said my blonde hair and blue eyes were highly accentuated when I wore shades of red, green, or deep blue. I wondered if I'd be able to find anything in velvet. Most of all, I wondered if I'd be able to find a dress I really loved at a price I could afford.

When we got in the store, we were really surprised to find a good selection of dresses. Nancy seemed drawn to a cream-colored dress with a chiffon overskirt, which I didn't think would look right on her, but I didn't say anything. Tina immediately started waving her arms around, calling out for us to look at this and that. I was afraid she was going to knock something over and embarrass us all. Tina found a pale-blue dress with iridescent sequins and was the first to head for the dressing room. I found a low-cut, forest-green dress with sheer forest-green sleeves and headed to the dressing room with Nancy, who was still clutching that cream-colored dress. We went into separate stalls and emerged to admire ourselves in the three-way mirror at the end of the dressing-room hallway. Nancy's dress looked stunning on her after all, and I loved the way mine looked, too. Mine fit like a glove. "Wow, we're princesses!" I said, and we laughed and twirled around, admiring ourselves from every angle.

Tina, who was apparently slow at dressing, came out in her blue dress and took her turn before the mirror, while Nancy and I assured her the blue dress was great. "Well, are we going to buy these or look more?" she asked.

"Let's get someone to hold these while we look more," I suggested. I did not want the shopping trip to be over so soon, so we found a clerk and had her hold our selections.

When Tina left us to try on a second dress, I told Nancy I enjoyed looking, but I planned to buy the green dress. "It's only seventy-nine dollars," I explained, "and it will be cold, so I'll probably have to buy some kind of shawl as well, if I don't want to freeze." I left her to look at dresses while I headed to another department in search of a suitable wrap to wear with the dress.

I couldn't believe my luck. I found a forest-green shawl in faux cashmere that had been marked down to fifteen dollars. I went back to show it to Nancy, but she saw me first, grabbed my arm, and said, "Look who's here." I glanced up and saw Wanda heading our way.

"Shopping for homecoming dresses?" Wanda asked.

I nodded, wishing she'd go away.

"You might want to save your money, because I've heard David still carries the torch for his ex-girlfriend."

"Don't tell her that shit," Nancy said. "Haven't you told enough lies already?"

Wanda shrugged and said, "Think what you will." She headed straight for the same dress I had chosen.

"Don't pick that one unless you want to be my twin," I said.

"Your twin? Oh, ha, ha, ha. I'm not looking for a dress *here*. To me, that would be like shopping at Kmart. I just want to see what kind of designer knock offs other girls will be wearing."

"Kiss my ass."

"Mine, too," Nancy said.

Wanda had gone by the time Tina came out of the dressing room. She was wearing a yellow dress that reminded me of Belle's dress from Disney's *Beauty and the Beast.* She gave a flourish down her sides while wiggling fingers on both hands. "What do you think?" she asked.

"Get the blue one," Nancy and I said in unison.

Chapter 6

The Royal Shaft

The first thing Monday morning I called the public health department office in Roanoke and made an appointment to see a doctor about getting some birth control pills. It turned out they had an opening and could see me that same afternoon, so I cut classes and borrowed Tina's car, promising to fill the gas tank before I returned.

The health department was in a red-brick building in the old downtown section of the city. I found a parking place and went inside. I had to ask a receptionist which office I needed, and she looked up at me with the most bored expression I've ever seen on a human being. "Follow the green tile hallway until you get to the double doors, and take a left; first door on the right," she said.

The gynecology office was just as drab as the rest of the building, with the same tiles and same pale-gray walls. The place smelled like disinfectant, but I supposed that meant it was clean. Another bored-looking receptionist told me to sign in and wait until my name was called. I sat in one of the green vinyl-covered, straight-back chairs that lined the walls. There were no magazines, but there were a few brochures on topics such as teen pregnancy. I was almost desperate enough to read one by the time a nurse called my name.

I followed the gray-haired woman into an examination room. She had permanent frown lines on her face, and an I-just-ate-a-sour-apple expression. She took my weight and told me to sit while she checked my blood pressure and temperature. I felt a lot of bad vibes from this woman, so I finally asked, "Are you having a bad day, or something?"

I saw her body stiffen. She flashed a fake smile and said, "I just don't like dealing with all the little whores that come through these doors—you know, girls like yourself, who never keep their legs closed." She shoved a yellow paper gown into my hands and said, "If you have any decency at all, put this on before the doctor comes in." Then she turned and left the room. I sat there kind of in shock. I couldn't believe it, but I knew this wasn't the time to take the high road. I would report her. I didn't want her talking to other girls like that. I went behind a curtain and changed into the gown.

The doctor was a fat, balding man who appeared to be in his sixties. To my dismay, the gray-haired nurse followed him when he came into the exam room. "Does she have to be here?" I asked.

"Yes, ma'am, she does. It's for my safety and yours. Doctors can take advantage and patients can make false accusations, but we won't have any of that today, will we?"

I sat up straight, trying to look as dignified as possible in my paper gown. "No, but I'd rather you get someone else. Your nurse just called me a whore."

"I did nothing of the sort," the nurse said. "I had to leave the room for a moment to get a thermometer with a battery that worked. When I came back she was pilfering through those drawers as if she were looking for something to steal."

For a moment, I was just dumbfounded. I couldn't believe she'd accuse me like that. I guess I'd classed Wanda into a separate category since she was my age. It finally hit me that liars come in all shapes, sizes, and ages.

"What were you looking for?" the doctor asked.

I found my voice and said, "Nothing! She's lying. She never left the room."

The doctor shook his head and said, "Let's get through your exam. We can sort this out later." I could tell he believed his nurse. I wanted so badly to walk out, but I thought of David and how I needed protection if I planned to be intimate with him. It was extremely humiliating to submit to the pelvic exam after all of that, but I did it for David.

My dad called in the middle of the week, and I told him about my dress and kept rambling on about David and the upcoming dance. He said he was glad I had gotten the dress and was very happy because I was happy. I told him it was almost time for pompom squad practice, and he said, "Sam, I called to tell you that I've decided to ask Carol to marry me."

I was caught off guard and didn't know what to say. Then I realized I was creating an awkward silence, so I said, "That's great, Dad. Congratulations."

He laughed and said, "Too early for congrats; she hasn't said yes yet."

"She'll say yes." *Of course she'll say yes.* I wondered what he saw in my old swim coach from the seventh grade.

He said, "Sam, there's one more thing." There was an awkward silence on Dad's part. I thought, *Oh God, please don't let him say Carol's knocked up.* Finally, he said, "You know I don't have a lot of money. I was wondering how you'd feel if I had the diamonds from your mother's wedding rings reset into a ring for Carol." My dad had lost his job as a welder when the company he had worked for had closed. He had been driving a bread truck for more than a year, while trying to find a better job. Nothing had opened up for him except an occasional odd job.

I heard myself say, "No problem, Dad," while inwardly I was screaming, *No! Mom's rings should be mine!*

I was so glad I hadn't said what I'd been thinking, because he said, "Thanks, Sam. I'm really proud of you." I could tell he meant it, and I suddenly knew I'd never have to do another thing to make Dad proud of me. *If I flunk out of school, he'll still be proud of me. If I become a crack addict, he'll still be proud of me. I can cross the goal of making Dad proud of me off my list.* I felt as if I'd just grown three inches taller or something.

"When are you going to ask her?" I asked, suddenly feeling more in the spirit of the idea.

"Soon."

After we hung up, I thought of Mom's rings. Her engagement ring had a half-carat round diamond in the center, with smaller round diamonds on each side. Her wedding ring was a thin yellow-gold band with three small pave-set diamonds. The three diamonds on each ring were supposed to represent today, tomorrow, and forever. I wiped a single tear from my left eye. Mom's forever had been cut short. I suddenly felt foolish for assuming my dad would eventually give me those rings. I guess he had no idea they were almost sacred to me. *The main thing is that he has a chance to be happy again.* I thought of David and the song

"You Are the Woman," and I smiled. *Dad and I both have the chance to be happy*, I thought.

When I got to pompom squad practice, it felt cold in the gymnasium. Most of us were wearing T-shirts and stretchy pants because we never wore our green-and-white skirts and tops unless we were performing in front of a crowd. Pompoms littered the polished wooden floor. The girls were talking about the homecoming dance. We were going to work on a special dance routine for the homecoming week football game. Tammy was late, which was very unusual, so I announced that we'd wait five minutes to give her time to show up. While we waited, I told Hillary about my new dress and my fabulous trip to O'Grady's with David. Wanda was standing nearby, and I knew she could hear me, but I didn't care. I glanced over at her once, and it looked as if she were about to butt in and say something, but she didn't. Then Tammy arrived and showed us all some dance moves she wanted to incorporate into the routine. Near the end, she wanted us to do a move like a jumping jack with legs apart, arms up and apart, facing the crowd, and then to jump up while turning our bodies one hundred and eighty degrees to face away from the crowd in the same position. Then she suggested another jump and turn that would have us facing the crowd, followed by a series of shimmies that would end with each girl in a forward split on the ground, pompoms held high on the final beat of the music. "What do you think?" she asked the squad as a whole.

Wanda raised her hand, and said, "What if, after that first jump that puts us facing away from the crowd, we bend forward and give a little butt wiggle to add more visual interest? Men think it's sexy, and women usually find it funny or cute."

I didn't like the source, but I loved the idea. "Let's try it," I said, so Tammy started our music and we had Wanda come up and demonstrate what she had in mind for the whole group.

"Looks good to me," Tammy said.

We went through the whole dance routine a couple of times, and when Tammy cut the music off, I heard a loud wolf whistle. A tall, blond-haired guy was standing over by the bleachers watching us. I couldn't help but smile as I hurried over to tell him to get out.

After I explained that we didn't allow people to watch our practice sessions, he smiled at me and said, "I know that, but I couldn't take my eyes off of you." He extended his hand and said, "I'm Steve Corson."

I remembered the name. This was the guy David had mentioned, the one who didn't seem to like David for some reason, but he seemed charming. There was no way I wasn't going to shake his hand, so I did, and he asked, "What's your name?"

"Samantha Fredrich."

"I'll leave peaceably if you give me your phone number."

I said, "Sorry, but I already have a boyfriend. Will you leave peaceably anyway?"

Nancy and I went to the September 21 Gamma Nu meeting, happy to report that we were averaging around a hundred dollars in profits each week from popcorn sales at movie night. We had learned that there were currently six women and ten children living in the women's shelter. Clarissa had obtained the children's ages and clothing sizes, along with the women's sizes, from the director. If we continued to do this well, we expected to have at least fifteen hundred dollars to buy gifts for the women and children at the shelter after the final movie night, which was on December 10. We thought that should be enough to brighten their Christmas, especially since most of us would also donate some money toward the fund.

After some discussion, we realized that everyone wanted to do the shopping, but very few of us would have a lot of time during that final week of school, because we'd all have to study for our final exams. Clarissa made a motion to buy a pretty sweater for each woman and a toy for each child and to give the rest in the form of gift cards for everyone. Jane seconded the motion, and we all approved that plan. Nancy, as treasurer, would be responsible for the shopping, and Jane volunteered to help her. I was in a brighter mood and noticed I didn't see my sorority sisters as a bunch of sheep that day. It pleased me that we were doing something special for others.

Nancy was on and off with Rob. I could never figure out what was going on with them, so I stopped trying. I continued to see David once a week, and we usually talked on the phone at least once a day. However, the closer we got to midterms, the less I saw of David. I decided to just follow suit and give myself over to my studies. It turned out to be very good for my grades.

It wasn't until the Friday after midterms that David came up to my room after a date. He'd opted to get a quick meal at Hardee's on Friday night, and then he'd helped me and Nancy sell popcorn for movie night. It was getting too chilly to have the event outside, so they'd moved it into Langford Auditorium. When David arrived, he helped us set up to sell. The crowd was much smaller because of fall break. No classes would be held on Monday and Tuesday, so many students had already left campus, although we didn't have to leave. David mentioned that his parents would be at a local church on Sunday, where his dad was slated to be a guest speaker, and that he planned to go home with them for fall break. He asked if I'd like to go to church with him and hear his dad's sermon. I said, yes, of course, thinking it was a very positive sign if he wanted me to meet his family. We decided to meet at the bus stop on Larsen Street and take a bus to the church.

They showed *Teen Wolf* with Michael J. Fox that night, in honor of Halloween month. David and I were giggly and playful behind the counter at the popcorn booth. Throughout the movie, he kept pawing at me and pretending to bite my neck. "I'm going to leave if you two don't knock it off," Nancy threatened.

I pulled her aside and asked, "What are your plans for later? I want to invite David to our room."

"Rob and I are going to hit the bars. I can stay in his room tonight."

David walked me back to my dorm after we had cleaned the popcorn machine and dragged it back into a storage room. This time, he offered no objections when I invited him to come up to our room. I think he sort of turned into a werewolf that night. He had my clothes off within a few minutes. He held me for a long time, just touching me and kissing me, and then he asked if I had any protection. I was so happy to tell him I'd gotten the birth control pills after our date at O'Grady's. "Want to see my pill pack?" I asked.

"Later," he murmured, and he was inside me.

I wanted him to stay all night, but he wouldn't. Even so, he left me giddy with ripples of pleasure coursing through my body.

On Sunday morning, David didn't show up at the bus stop. I waited until nearly nine thirty and then walked back to my dorm. Nancy said he hadn't called.

"I could call his dorm and see if he forgot," I suggested.

"I think he should be the one doing the calling," she said. "He probably studied so late that he overslept."

I gave her a look of frustration and said, "This really sucks. I wanted to meet his family."

I studied for a couple of hours, and then Tina and Marsha dropped in to see whether we wanted to have lunch with them, so we all took off for the cafeteria. David wasn't there, either. After lunch, I went back to my room and found he had left a note on the door to apologize, so I forgave him. The note read, "Hi, Beautiful. Sorry about being AWOL for our date this morning. I forgot to set an alarm and overslept. Please forgive me. I was dreaming about you." I glanced at my watch and figured he had already left town with his parents. I was still disappointed, but I tried not to be upset with David. He had no way of knowing how much the chance to meet his parents had meant to me, at least I didn't think he did. I realized I was being silly. If his parents were destined to be my future in-laws, I would eventually meet them.

That afternoon, Nancy and I borrowed Tina's car and went to Salem to pick up her old high-school boyfriend, Brad, from home. I had no idea why she wanted to see him, but I didn't want to pry. I wondered if things had soured with Rob. Brad ended up staying with her overnight, so I slept in our study room on her folding canvas recliner. Before I went to sleep, David called to apologize and to let me know he'd arrived home safely. He said he'd call when he got back to campus.

On Monday morning, Brad got some guy he knew on campus to take him home. "What was that all about?" I asked.

"Just two old friends getting reacquainted," she said.

"In bed? Yeah, right."

Nancy just smiled. We were both cheerful, and I started talking with Nancy about how much I liked David and how excited I was about the homecoming dance. Then our phone rang. We couldn't decide who should answer it, but finally she did. "It's for you," she said, handing me the receiver. I was surprised because I hadn't given many people my number.

"Samantha, I'm David's girlfriend," a shrill voice said at the other end of the line. "You can forget everything he said to you and all that's happened between you. He's mine."

"Who is this?" I asked, wondering if Wanda had put someone up to this.

"I'm his future wife," she said. "We're engaged now. You can ask him yourself. After that, stay away from him."

I couldn't believe it. But then, who would tell a lie like that and suggest I ask David to verify it? Then I thought, *David must have given her my phone number. What an ass!* I found my voice and said, "You can both just go to hell!" and hung up.

I was angry and hurt. When I get mad, I usually cry, even though I don't want to. I stood there with tears running down my face, cussing and explaining what had happened. At times like this I really loved Nancy. She just looked at me, with her blue eyes darkening, and said, "Well, that stinkin' son of a bitch!" She took me to Hardee's to cheer me up, but it didn't help. When we got back, our sorority sisters were going on a jock raid. I went along, hoping it would cheer me up, but it didn't.

David never called me on Tuesday, but I assumed he was back on campus. On Wednesday night, I saw him in the cafeteria, and I said, "I got a very strange phone call yesterday. Are you engaged?"

He sighed and said, "It's complicated." He appeared very uncomfortable, but I didn't care. I wanted a straight answer.

"No, it's not. You're either engaged or you're not." Several people turned to look at us, and I realized I was talking loudly. I lowered my voice. "Are you?" I asked.

He looked down at his plate of spaghetti and said, "Yes."

I felt like slapping the hell out of him, but I just said, "That's all I wanted to know" and immediately turned away. I wanted him to call me back to him and say it had been some stupid, half-assed joke, but he didn't. My legs felt kind of weak while I walked toward the exit, as if my knees were about to buckle. I couldn't keep the tears from coming down my cheeks. It's hard to explain exactly how I felt, but it was a combination of hurt, anger, and a sense of my own foolishness for being so easily taken by David's charm. Above all, I felt a sense of humiliation. I was having a hard time seeing through my tears, and I didn't want to draw attention to them by wiping at my eyes, so I made my way as quickly as I could across the beige tiled floor. Then, to my horror, I almost walked into Wanda in my haste to leave.

Chapter 7

Changing Plans

When Nancy came in from dinner, she found me stuffing the dress and shawl I'd bought for the homecoming dance into a shopping bag. "What are you doing?" she demanded. She pushed me gently into a sitting position on my bed and put the dress and shawl back on a hanger. "David isn't the only guy in the world," she said. "Why not find someone even better and go just to spite him? Who needs a boyfriend who can only see her once a week anyway? That's a bunch of crap."

I sat there and considered it for a few minutes. It was a bunch of crap, whether David had used the time to study or to get cozy with his fiancée. I just couldn't understand why he'd gone to so much trouble to impress me and make me feel special. It was really low of him to make me think he'd fallen for me at first sight, to sleep with me, and then to announce that he was engaged and say, "It's complicated." *What an asshole!* I started tearing up again because I felt so miserable.

Nancy helped a lot when she said, "I know I haven't shown the best track record for being emotionally strong, but if it were me, I'd get a date for the dance and act as though nothing major had happened. Who do you know that you could invite to the dance?"

At that moment, I remembered Steve Corson, who had crashed pompon squad practice and asked for my phone number—the guy who didn't like David. *Well, now we have something in common, because I don't like David either.* I picked up the phone and called campus information, asked for Steve's phone number, and jotted it on a scrap of paper. I was about to call him when Tina and Marsha dropped by. I must have looked pathetic, because Tina flung her hands out to her sides, palms up, and asked, "What's wrong?" I started crying again and told them the whole stinking mess. They both encouraged me to call Steve and ask him to the homecoming dance.

"What if he says no?" I asked.

"Then go by yourself and hold your head high," Marsha said, "but pin the price tag under and wear that dress carefully. Then return it the next day."

For some reason I found that hilarious and laughed until I nearly peed in my pants. Marsha kept saying, "What? What's so funny about that?"

"Nothing. Everything. You really *would* do something like that, wouldn't you?"

"Hell, yeah. If you end up going alone, that dress ain't going to have a lot of sentimental value after Saturday night."

Dad called that night to announce that Carol had said yes when he'd asked her to marry him, and I nearly burst into tears. I'd heard enough news about engagements recently. I managed to say, "That's great. I'm happy for you." He said the jeweler had called after lunch to say the rings were ready, and after he'd picked them up, he'd decided to propose over dinner. I asked what the engagement ring was like, and he said he'd just opted to have Mom's half-carat diamond mounted as a solitaire in white gold and that he'd purchased a three-millimeter plain white gold band to make it a set with a wedding ring. That kept it from looking so much like my mother's rings, he said. *And from being just as nice*, I thought with some satisfaction. I figured he would probably have the other diamonds mounted into some piece of jewelry to give Carol as a wedding gift, but I felt too miserable to ask about them. I'd had all the news I could stand.

"So, are you all set for homecoming?" Dad asked.

"I guess so," I lied. Then I broke down and told my dad about what had happened. I even told him I'd slept with David. "What do you make of it?"

"I don't know, but I'd like to beat his ass." We were both silent for a moment, and then Dad asked, "Do you want me to come up and take you to that dance?" as if that would fix everything.

"No, Dad. I'm sorry, but that would be a little too embarrassing. If I can't get another date, I probably just won't go."

"Keep your nose to the sky, Sam," he said before he hung up. That was a saying he'd made up for me when Carol was my swim coach in seventh grade and I'd come in dead last in three events at one swim meet.

"I will, Daddy."

It took a few tries, but I finally caught Steve on the phone later that night. "Hi, Steve," I said. "This is Samantha Fredrich from pompom squad. Do you remember me?"

"Are you the short, bowlegged girl with knobby knees?" he asked.

I giggled. "No, we don't have anyone like that on our squad."

"Okay, got it. Are you the girl with long black hair and a wart on her nose?"

I smiled and said, "Nope."

"Oh, I remember now. You're the girl with light brown hair and mysterious green eyes that I've been dying to go out with."

"That's me," I said.

"Is your boyfriend out of the picture?"

"Totally."

"Who was he, anyway?"

I was surprised that he didn't know. "His name was David Martin."

Steve laughed and said, "That asshole? I can't believe it."

"Neither can I." I paused a moment to get up my courage and said, "Steve, I find you very attractive. Would you consider going to the homecoming dance with me—if you don't already have a date, that is?"

"I'd love to, but it's just three days away. Would it be okay if I wear a suit if I have trouble lining up a tuxedo?"

"Of course. Wear whatever you want. I just want to have a good time." *And I want it to gall David to see me with you, if he shows up.*

"Cool. Hey, what are you doing tonight?"

Nancy left with Rob to hit the bars a little later, and I wondered whether Rob knew she'd spent a night with Brad. I doubted it. I planned to spend the evening studying, but they hadn't been gone long before my inner anguish returned. I knew I wouldn't be able to study effectively. Then Steve dropped by with a bouquet of burgundy mums and his books. We set up at the small desks in our study room, and I was actually able to get a lot accomplished on my political science homework assignment. Being with Steve kept the horrible feelings of hurt, anger, and humiliation at bay. I briefly wondered why David couldn't have studied with me over the past few weeks instead of sequestering himself, but I figured he must have been with his fiancée during much of the time.

I looked over at Steve, who was really too tall to be sitting at Nancy's desk, and admired the muscles in his arms and shoulders. He was every bit as good-looking as David was but in a different way. After an hour of studying, we went out for a walk around campus. I thought he might ask about my recent breakup, but he didn't. He asked about me and why I'd chosen Fermen and what I planned to do after graduation. I felt very comfortable with him and admitted I wouldn't have had the money to think about attending Fermen without my scholarship. He told me he was hoping to get into the premed program at Washington and Lee. *Just like David,* I thought.

I asked, "Are you building up to an explanation that you can't see me often because you have to study so much?"

"Not at all. What brought that on?"

I told him that David had claimed his academics were so challenging and competitive that he could only spend time with me once a week.

"That has nothing to do with academics. That's because he's a moron . . . well, actually he's smart, but I don't think he has enough confidence to just hang loose. Have you heard that expression, 'If you can't run with the big dogs, stay off the porch'? Anyone that uptight should stay off the porch. That's just my take on the situation. I told him if he didn't make it as a doctor, he could work as a PA in my medical office."

"What a PA?"

"You know—a physician's assistant."

"Do you know who he's engaged to?"

Steve stopped walking for a moment and asked, "If I answer that, can we stop talking about him forever?" I nodded, and he continued. "Some chick started driving us crazy right before break, trying to reach David on the dorm phone. He was never around when she called, and she kept leaving messages for him to call Sara. The calls stopped after spring break. That's all I know."

I wanted to ask if he'd told his friends he was engaged, but I'd promised to stop talking about David. "Tell me about you," I said.

Steve told me his father was an orthopedic physician in Roanoke. He said he'd chosen Fermen because he'd been offered a full scholarship and he wanted to save his dad some money. He was hoping to specialize in orthopedics as well, and his future college bills would likely be astronomical. We talked until nearly 1:00 a.m. before heading back to my room. Steve kissed me, and I didn't complain when he put his hands inside my sweater. We were in my bed by the time Nancy came in, so she took her blankets and pillow and headed for the canvas recliner in the study room. "No need to leave," Steve told her. "We're just snuggling and snoozing. Sleep in your bed."

Steve was gone when I woke up the next morning, but I nearly stumbled over his chemistry book, which he'd apparently forgotten. I smiled because I knew he'd have to come back and pick it up soon.

Chapter 8

The Big Game

Pompom squad practice and all the preparations for homecoming didn't leave me a lot of time to dwell on my sorrows. Sure, my eyes still became teary several times over the next few days, but I tried to shrug off all negative emotion. If I'd had time, I might have curled into a ball and hibernated for a while. By Friday, the day of the homecoming football game, word of what had happened between David and me had spread throughout Gamma Nu and the pompom squad as well. When I went to our final practice on the day of the game, I eyed Wanda to see if there was any hint of mockery in her eyes, but I didn't find any. I'd have wanted to punch her if she'd said, "I told you so." I knew that Wanda was on the homecoming court, along with Clarissa and Danna, from Gamma Nu, and a girl named Sharon. I wondered how Wanda had known about David's other girlfriend and decided to ask her when I got a chance. We went through our dance routine several times without any problems, so we felt very confident that we would put on a good show at the football game later that evening. Everyone else seemed very excited, but I found it hard to care who would win the game between the Fermen Bulldogs and the Lenton College Bears.

I went to my political science class after practice and nearly nodded off. I liked Professor Harmon, but I found it very hard to pay attention to him that day. I think half the class was having the same problem, for different reasons, and Harmon must have realized that, too, because he let everyone go twenty minutes early. I grabbed a sandwich and went back to the dorm, where I found Nancy in bed with some guy I'd never seen before. I wondered why she wasn't in class. I closed our bedroom door and went to sit in our study room. Nancy had already announced that she didn't care about the football game, so I hoped she wouldn't be holed up in bed all day and all night. I'd eventually have to go in there to get my pompom squad outfit.

Steve dropped a few minutes later to let me know he'd been able to rent a tuxedo for the dance after all. "I stuck with plain black and white to be safe," he said. "I don't want us clashing." I felt a sudden rush of fondness for Steve, understanding that he'd gone to considerable expense for our date. "I was thinking about dinner tomorrow night," he said. "I know you don't have a lot of extra cash, so why not let me make it special? Have you ever been to O'Grady's?"

"Once," I said. He must have read my look, because he immediately started telling me about Shepherd's, another great place he knew in Roanoke. "Sounds perfect . . . and thanks," I said.

The Fermen Bulldogs were ahead 18-7 at halftime. The cheerleaders came out and did a special routine, and I noticed Wanda watching them with a wistful look on her face. I wondered how much she regretted being off their team, since she had been the one that had pointed out to me that the pompom squad girls weren't *real* cheerleaders. *We're more like a dance team,* I thought. *No shame in that.* I knew it had been too late for her dad to fix that when he'd come to her rescue last semester. There were fourteen spots on the cheerleading team, and Wanda's spot had been filled with an alternate promptly upon her dismissal. I still felt that her dismissal should never have been reversed and changed to probation.

The marching band performed, and then it was time for our pompom squad routine. It felt great to perform while the crowd was so pumped and everyone seemed to be in a good mood—well, everyone but the Lions fans on the other side of the stadium. After we finished, an emcee introduced the homecoming court, and I was shocked to see David escorting the girl named Sharon onto the court. I knew she couldn't be his fiancée, but I had no idea what their connection was. It stung to see him walking her out onto center field, and whatever enthusiasm I'd picked up from the crowd evaporated. Wanda was crowned homecoming queen, as I had expected. As much I as hated to admit it, she was drop-dead gorgeous. *But not on the inside, where it matters most,* I thought. I stayed with the squad throughout the second half, but I felt like a lost child. I wished so much that Steve would show up and take me somewhere, anywhere. The Bulldogs held on to the lead, and the game ended 31-19.

After the game, I decided to take a walk on campus, and I headed for the section near the classroom buildings and library, away from the crowd. I found Wanda in the shadows under the oak trees behind Jackson Hall. "I thought you'd be hitting the bars with your friends," I said, allowing some of my distaste for her to show.

"That was my thing last year," she said, "but not now. My dad made me go into an alcohol rehab program before he'd agree to do anything to help me get back in school." She lit a cigarette, and I saw a tear slide down her cheek.

"That means he loves you," I said.

"Yeah, maybe, but if he does, I never knew it when I was a little girl. Maybe he's afraid I'll just be an embarrassment to him. I wanted him to be proud of me."

She took a drag of her cigarette. I was touched to see that Wanda and I shared at least one goal of making our dads proud. We stood there silently for a few minutes, and then she said, "I fucked my way through all of my father's friends and most of his enemies just to get even with him for ignoring me when I was a child." Then she threw the cigarette down and started crying in earnest. I didn't know what to say. I finally put a hand on her shoulder, and Wanda just broke down completely. I pulled her close to me and held her as if she were a child. When she settled down, I released her, and she wiped her tears away and said, "Life goes on."

As I walked back to the dorm, a cold rain began to fall. *Does life go on?* I wondered. I found that giving some comfort to Wanda had only staved off my feelings of emptiness and sorrow for a few moments. I was drenched by the time I got back to my room. I called Steve and found he'd opted to study instead of going to the game. I asked if he could come over. "Sure, what's up?" he asked.

"I'm cold," I said, and I started to cry.

Chapter 9

The Homecoming Dance

At six o'clock, Nancy and I were almost ready to go out. We'd showered and helped each other with hairstyling. She'd helped me create a nice French twist, and I'd crimped her hair. We'd moved to our separate dressers and started doing our own makeup. I was putting coppery eye shadow on my lids when I heard Nancy yell, "Shit!"

She'd dropped her mascara wand and gotten smudges of black mascara on the bodice and front panel of her cream-colored dress. I ran over to her, and she looked as though she were about to burst into tears, which would make an even bigger mess. "It's okay. Hang on. I think I can fix it," I said. I grabbed a can of dry shampoo off my dresser, sprayed one of the smudge marks, and headed to our bathroom to get a damp washcloth. We let the dry shampoo set for a minute before I wiped it off. "It worked," I said, and she sat there staring at the clean spot for a moment and blinking, as if I'd done a magic trick.

"Thanks," she said.

I quickly sprayed the other smudges, and we had her dress back to normal in minutes. Tina and Marsha came in, looking beautiful. Tina was wearing the pale-blue dress with iridescent sequins, and she had worked tiny baby's breath flowers into her hair, which was pulled up into a loose bun. Marsha wore a deep-purple satin dress with a bow at the waist. I hoped Tina's date was tall, because she'd emphasized her height by wearing spikey heels. "We're princesses!" she said, flinging her arms toward the ceiling and twirling around in her dress.

"Won't you be uncomfortable in those?" I asked.

Tina giggled and opened a little silver handbag to reveal a small hairbrush, a lipstick, and two odd looking wads. "Ballet slippers," she said. "I found I could roll them up and make them fit in my purse."

Marsha said, "Damn, I wish I had thought of that." Marsha and Tina left as abruptly as they'd arrived, and there was a knock on the door. This time it was a floral delivery, two packages from the same shop: a wrist corsage of white carnations for me and a pink one for Nancy, from Steve and Rob. I had forgotten about corsages and wasn't expecting one, so I was very pleased that Steve had sent one for me.

About five minutes later Rob showed up, and I snapped photos of him and Nancy before they took off for a fancy Chinese restaurant. Steve arrived a few minutes later, looking great in his black tuxedo. We admired one another for a moment, giving compliments, and then he said, "I have bad news for you. I wasn't able to get reservations at Shepherd's. We'll have to go somewhere else."

On a whim, I said, "We could have beanie weenies and potato chips right here. I have a little hotplate in the closet."

"I thought those were illegal in the dorms."

"They are."

"I love beanie weenies," he said, so I took the hotplate out and plugged it in. I dumped a couple of cans of beanie weenies into a pot and put it on to heat. "There's a bag of potato chips on top of that little refrigerator," I told him. When I turned around, he was stripping.

"What are you doing?"

"I can't risk getting beanie weenies on these clothes," he said, and I watched him strip down to his underwear.

"So what if we'd gone to a restaurant?" I asked.

"I have this beach towel I use as a bib," he joked.

I took off my dress, and we sat on the floor and ate beanie weenies from Styrofoam bowls with plastic forks, sharing a bag of potato chips and washing it all down with cans of Coke. As an afterthought, I got up, lit a candle and set it on the floor between us.

Light reflected off several disco balls on the ceiling in the ballroom at Stanton Hall that evening. I was surprised to see that the student activity union had also hired the band Red Dawg for this event. I felt a twinge of sorrow when I saw the band, because it brought back memories of the night I'd met David. I looked at Steve and tried to forget that other night with David. Steve and I had punch and sampled hors d'oeuvres that were far better than our dinner, until Nancy and Marsha waved for us to come and sit at their table. "Where'd you guys go for dinner?" Nancy asked.

"A place called Beenitos," Steve said. "It was great."

Marsha frowned and said, "I don't know where that is."

"It's not far from here. You should try it," I said. I took Steve's hand and said, "Let's dance." When we came back to the table, Marsha was dancing with someone, Nancy and Rob were talking, and Beenitos was forgotten. Steve leaned in toward me and asked if I minded if he danced with others, and I said no, that I'd do the same. He headed off toward a group of people, and I sat, content to watch the crowd.

About fifteen minutes later, an emcee came to the stage and announced that he'd like to introduce the homecoming court. I was unprepared for that. Moments later, Wanda and her court were headed to the stage, and there was David with Sharon on his arm. I suddenly felt as if I couldn't get enough air. Nancy patted my hand to offer support, but I said, "I need to get out of here."

Outside, I stepped onto a patio that wrapped around the building. There were a few people milling around near the entrance, so I kept walking until I'd turned the corner, where it was darker. This section of the patio appeared deserted, so sat on a bench in the shadows and started crying softly. When I'd settled down a bit, I felt a soft hand on my shoulder and looked up. "He isn't worth it, you know," Wanda said, and she handed me a tissue.

When I'd regained my composure, I asked, "So what designer label are you wearing tonight?" I could see the quality in the royal-blue gown she was wearing.

Wanda shook her head and said, "Who knows? Haven't you caught on to me yet? This is just a dress I wore for my cousin's wedding last year."

"Why didn't you get a new one?"

"Because I didn't give a shit." She patted me on the shoulder and said, "Let's go in and fix your makeup."

I shook my head and said, "I think I need to go home."

She said, "No, you don't. He's already left, if that's what you're worried about. He just made an appearance for his cousin's sake. I have no idea why Sharon didn't invite a real date."

I followed her to the ladies' room and stood by the mirror while she moistened tissues and wiped at the mascara my tears had smudged around my eyes. When she saw I didn't have my purse, she asked, "Are you afraid to use some of mine? They say it isn't sanitary, you know." I shook my head and looked up so she could brush mascara onto my lashes. She took out some of her eye pencils and lined my eyes, stood back and studied me, and then added an extra touch of blush to my cheeks. I was amazed at how glamorous I looked when she was done. She turned to go, but I stopped her and said, "Thanks."

"No problem."

Before she left, I asked, "How did you know David had another girlfriend?"

"Because the crazy bitch called my boyfriend's dorm night and day looking for him. I answered the phone one day and told her he had a girlfriend on campus, and she said, "He *will* come back to me.' She said it with so much assurance that I believed her."

I started to ask another question, but Wanda cut me off with, "That's all I know."

Back in the ballroom, I found Steve, who did a double take when he saw me. "Are you *my* date?" he asked. "You look even more gorgeous."

"Thanks. I just took a trip to the powder room and found my fairy godmother."

Steve had apparently been having a great time. I'm not even sure he realized I had left the ballroom for nearly half an hour. I thought of what Wanda had said the night before, 'Life goes on,' so I decided to have a good time. Steve introduced me to his roommate, George, who immediately asked me to dance. "If that's all right with you," he said, looking at Steve.

"Sure, she's free game. She's my date, not my girl."

I didn't like the way that sounded, but I smiled and took George's hand, thinking, *Free game? I'll show him what "free game" is.* George turned out to be a very nice guy, but he wasn't as cute as Steve was. He was only a couple of inches taller than I was, and I wasn't wearing heels, so I guessed he was about five-seven. At least he had beautiful eyes—dark brown with long lashes most girls would envy. His hair was a mass of soft black curls. I wondered if he was Hispanic. By the end of the evening, I had danced with about a dozen guys. Steve and I had only danced together twice. I felt exhausted and tired of playing games. I wanted someone to hold me, but I was too proud to ask Steve to come up to my room.

Chapter 10

A Downhill Slide

By the next week, all my pride had vanished. It wasn't so much Steve's announcement that I was his date, not his girl, as it was something in the back of my mind that kept screaming and demanding to know why David had abandoned me. Steve's easy way of leaving my side to be with others made me wonder if every guy I ever liked would find me easy to walk away from.

Steve and I spent a lot of time together in the days following the dance, and by Halloween I felt as if I had "imprinted" on Steve and needed to be near him as much as a duckling needs to follow its mother. It came to me that sex might bring us closer together and make him think of me as "his girl."

On Monday, the day after Halloween, some guy dropped by and asked for Nancy. I told him to wait a moment while I went to get her. "What the hell are you doing?" I asked. "Trying to screw every guy on campus? I thought you were back with Rob."

She shrugged and said, "Rob, Schmob," and then she left. It seemed that Nancy and I were on opposite ends of the spectrum in our thinking about men. When Rob called a little later, I didn't have the heart to tell him she was with someone else. After I hung up the phone, I started feely panicky and flighty. I felt men were treating me like Nancy treated men. It's hard to explain the exact mix of emotions, but I needed someone or something, and I wasn't sure what.

I called Steve and asked him to come over. As soon as he got there, I kissed him and put my hand on his dick. "I want you inside me," I said. "Now."

Soon we were writhing on my bed, and he was rough. I guess he thought if I could be demanding then he could, too. When we stopped and cuddled for a while, it almost felt like love.

For the next couple of weeks, I either slept in Steve's room or he slept in mine. I only seemed to feel right when I had his arms around me, but I knew that wasn't healthy. When I told Nancy I felt that way, she asked, "Are you losing you mind?" She suggested I'd get over it if I'd get my "head out of Steve's ass."

By the time Thanksgiving drew near, I was managing to keep my grades together because Steve frequently studied with me. I could study all night if he was beside me; I just couldn't do it if I was alone. Dad called to check on me on the Friday before Thanksgiving, and I told him I wanted to ask Steve to come home with me for Thanksgiving. He said that would be fine. Dad seemed incredibly happy for a change. He kept telling me what a great meal we were going to have, since Carol would be cooking. I secretly hoped it wouldn't be as nice as my mom's Thanksgiving dinners.

The next day, Nancy, Marsha, Tina, and I were having lunch with Steve, Rob, and George in the cafeteria when a guy named Marshall came over and started talking to Rob. He was a bear of a guy, who looked as if he would make a great lineman for a football team. Rob introduced everyone, and when he came to me, Marshall blurted out, "Man, she's beautiful. I'd like to ask her out."

Steve said, "Well, ask her, dude. She's not seeing anyone."

My mouth dropped open, but I couldn't find any words for a moment. I felt heat rising in my cheeks. George defused the moment with, "The hell she's not. She's mine," and the others laughed.

Later, George pulled me aside and told me not to take what Steve had said to heart. "He's trying to play it cool," he said, "but I know he thinks a lot of you."

I made up my mind to get out more and see other people, so when Tina invited me and Nancy to a "girl's night out" on the day before Thanksgiving break, I said yes. We all put on opaque black pantyhose with ultra-short dresses before heading out. Once we got in Tina's car, she suggested we go all the way to a nightclub called The Dragon's Den, in Roanoke. Tina had heard that one of her favorite bands, Maced, was playing there. When we got inside and found a table, we ordered a pitcher of beer. I was just starting to relax when Tina nudged me and said, "Isn't that Steve?"

Sure enough, Steve was sitting at a table across on the other side of the dance floor with an inebriated blonde in his lap. "Do you want to go somewhere else?" Tina asked, which was gracious, considering we'd just paid to get in and we would still have to pay for the beer.

"No, let's just ignore him," I said. I moved to the chair that put my back to Steve, said, "Steve, Schmeve" and tried to give a convincing smile. Inside, I felt panicky and lost. Although it was full of people, the place felt cold to me, maybe because of the wisps of fog from the dry ice used on the stage.

When the server arrived with our beer pitcher and three frosted mugs, he poured our first round carefully, leaving very little head. I tried to chug mine and nearly made it, but I had to breathe once before drinking the last bit. Tina and Nancy and giggled tried to chug theirs, too. We ordered another round and tried again. Tina actually succeeded on her second try.

By this time we'd drawn some attention to ourselves, and people at the tables around us were laughing with us. A guy in cowboy boots and a gray T-shirt, who appeared to be about thirty, bought us a third pitcher because, as he said, "I'd gladly pay seven dollars to see that again." Of course, we felt obligated to repeat the performance, and it wasn't long until I was happily drunk.

After we finished that pitcher, I flagged him over, pointed toward Steve, and whispered, "See that guy with the girl in his lap?"

He nodded.

"That's my boyfriend. I want to do what she's doing with him, with you."

"All right."

I stood up and pointed to a chair across from me. When he sat down, I straddled his lap and kissed him. When I stopped, he said, "Damn, what's your name, darlin'?"

I belched and said, "Samantha."

"Nice to meet you, Samantha. I'm Thurman . . . by the way, you just wasted a good fart, honey." I laughed as if that were the funniest thing I'd ever heard in my life. I could tell that, even drunk, Nancy and Tina didn't think much of Thurman or his humor, and that made me laugh even harder.

I pretended to be enthralled with Thurman. "Could I have your phone number?" I asked, and I saw Nancy roll her eyes.

Thurman patted me on the thigh and said, "You'd better just enjoy what you can of me tonight. My old lady will be home tomorrow." I didn't bother to ask where his "old lady" was that night.

Thurman lifted a sleeve on his T-shirt to show me his latest tattoo, a Confederate flag. "I'm going to get a portrait of Robert E. Lee when I get the money," he said.

I put my arms around Thurman and asked, "Do you think my boyfriend is jealous yet?" Thurman tipped a glance toward Steve and said, "Nope, we need to try harder."

I traced the lines under his eyes with my fingertips and noticed a bit of gray was starting to show at his temples. I frowned and said, "Excuse me, Thurman Thompson, but I have to pee really bad."

When I went to the restroom, Tina was standing by the sinks when I came out of a stall. She held her hands palms up, fingers curled, and bounced them while asking, "What are you doing with that redneck?"

"I don't know," I said, and I started to cry.

Chapter 11

Thanksgiving

I was glad to see Dad when he came to pick me up for Thanksgiving break. He appeared happier and more settled than he had seemed in a long time. I suppose Dad was too happy to notice my state of lower energy. Steve had never indicated he'd even noticed my presence at the Dragon's Den the night before, and he hadn't called. I was miserable about that, miserable about having David desert me, and miserable to think that no one would ever really care about me. Even so, I was glad that Dad was happy.

"I have a surprise for you," he said when we reached the house. He took my bag and unlocked the front door. I didn't see anything different, and there were no gift boxes in sight.

"What's the surprise?"

"You remember how we talked about you not being a little girl anymore when you brought that fella home last year? Well, I started thinking about that again, so I updated your bedroom for you. No more unicorns prancing across the walls. Go take a look."

I ran upstairs and found my walls were now a shade called "Mermaid's Dream," which was written on the lid of an empty paint can in my empty closet. It was a beautiful pale, blue-green. A new bedspread and curtains finished the look. "Carol helped me pick it out after I told her which colors you like," he said. "She made the curtains and throw pillows herself."

"Thank you. I love it, and I'll be sure to thank her as well."

For an instant, something swelled in me, and I felt almost as if I had my mom back. It was nice to have someone who would do something like that for me.

I didn't see Carol until Thanksgiving Day, when I awakened to the scent of spicy pumpkin pies baking in the oven and went downstairs to investigate. Carol had cooked a huge turkey at her house the night before. She had various things going on the stove. I peeked in the oven and saw three pies. "Looks like you're cooking for an army," I said.

"Well, sort of. Did you father tell you my parents are coming over?"

I cringed inwardly and said, "No, but that's great. By the way, thanks for helping revamp my room. I love the curtains and throw pillows you made."

She smiled, obviously pleased that I'd brought it up. "You're quite welcome."

I started working beside her, peeling the skin off baked potatoes and mashing them up for a casserole. I washed pots and pans, set the dining room table, and generally tried to help her make things nice. While washing a set of measuring spoons, I noticed her engagement ring on the windowsill above the sink, and she must have seen me staring at it. "Beautiful, isn't it?" she asked.

"Mind if I try it on?"

"Not at all."

I slipped the ring onto my finger and turned it this way and that in the light. It was beautiful and nicer than an ordinary diamond solitaire in that the six-prong mountings twisted to give the ring some extra flair.

Dad came into the kitchen while I was looking at it and asked, "Like it, Sam?" He walked over to peek in the oven and give Carol a quick kiss. For a little while, I forgot to worry about my own pathetic love life. I even forgot to brace myself against the arrival of Carol's parents, which turned out to be needless. They were charming, elegant people.

I lay on my bed late in the afternoon, looking at my Mermaid's Dream walls and new curtains. In this environment, happiness didn't seem so elusive. I didn't know what was going on with Steve or why David had dumped me, but for a little while I felt buffered from all of that. I felt that things might somehow work out well for me, after all.

That night, I got a long-distance phone call from Danna. "Guess what?" she said. "I saw a wedding announcement in the Richmond News today. David is married!"

I felt my stomach lurch as if I'd just gone down the first big hill on a roller coaster. "Married to who?"

"To Miss Deanna Lynn Summers of Hanover, VA." She read the whole clipping to me:

Miss Deanna Lynn Summers and Mr. David Robert Martin were united in marriage Sunday, November 21, 1999 at four thirty in the afternoon at Morning Star

Community Church in Hanover, Virginia. The bride is the daughter of Mr. and Mrs. Melvin Summers of Hanover, VA. The groom is the son of Rev. and Mrs. John Martin, of Richmond, VA. The ceremony was officiated by the father of the groom. Wedding and reception music was provided by Sharon Hamilton, cousin of the groom.

The bride is a 1997 graduate of Hanover High School and is currently working as a receptionist at Waldorf Medical Center in Hanover. The groom is a 1997 graduate of Thomas Jefferson High School in Richmond, VA. He is currently attending Fermen College in Vinton, VA.

Matron of Honor was Emma Sanders, from Hanover, VA. Bridesmaids were Jennifer Thompson, Lauren Jenkins, Leanna Tiswell, and Katie Nelson, all from Hanover, VA. Flower girl was Bella Johnson, from Hanover.

Best man was Timothy Hamilton, of Richmond, VA. Groomsmen were Tommy Summers and Jeff Summers, brothers of the bride, from Hanover, VA; Marshall Stratton, from Reedy Creek, VA; and Isaac Wallace, from Rocky Knob, VA. Ring bearer was Todd Weston, from Richmond.

Program and guest book attendant was Kaye Sharp.

The bride wore a traditional gown with a sweetheart neckline, an elegant beaded bodice, back button details, and a chapel train. She also wore a strand of pearls, a gift from the groom.

A celebration followed the ceremony at the Hanover Country Club. The couple is honeymooning in Orlando, Florida and will make their home in Hanover, VA.

I was slightly sick and numb by the time she read all of that. I thought, *David is honeymooning in Florida with that shrill-voiced bitch right this moment!* Just based on the length of the wedding announcement, it seemed that wedding must have been in the works for a long time. The other part that got me was "a strand of pearls, a gift from the groom." I missed part of what Danna was saying while considering that.

"—whatever. Well, I don't know if you wanted to hear that or not, but I thought you'd rather hear it from a friend if you had to hear it at all."

I sighed and said, "Thanks for letting me know." As an afterthought, I asked, "Is there a picture? What does she look like?"

"Well, she's okay, not that great. She looks a little chunky to me. She has dark hair and a big, horsey smile."

We giggled over the "big horsey smile" for a moment, but it was a cheerless giggle on my part. I figured anyone who married David Martin would have a big horsey smile. How I wished he'd married me.

That evening I kept going through things in my mind in an endless loop. I couldn't help but wonder if he'd ever played "You Are the Woman" for Deanna Summers when he was romancing her. I couldn't make sense of it. Why would he act so crazy about me if he were planning to marry that girl? Why wouldn't he just tell me himself if he wanted to break off our relationship? Why be such a chickenshit? Was he born an asshole, or did he practice all his life? Why would he get married if he were hoping to enter a premed program? I wondered all that and more. I wished I could slide into bed with Steve and cuddle up. Maybe then I could sleep. It was a big mistake to think about that, because that sent me off wondering why *he* couldn't be happy with me. Why did he need to have that other girl in his lap at the Dragon's Den? I was on the pompom squad. I was reasonably attractive and in good physical shape. I wondered, *What does it take to hold on to a guy? Is something wrong with me?*

I had Dad and Carol take me back to campus the next day. It wasn't what they'd planned, but Carol said she'd like to go shopping in Roanoke anyway. I did this because I just couldn't stand the idea of making Dad and Carol miserable because I was miserable, and I didn't want them to know anything was wrong. I made an excuse about needing to study, and we took off. On the ride back, I pretended to read my history book the whole way so I wouldn't have to make small talk.

Chapter 12

A Little Help from My Friends

Campus was quiet, so I mostly slept through the rest of Thanksgiving break. When classes started again on November 29, I was in zombie mode. I went through the motions of going to class, meetings, and campus events. The only thing that made me feel better was the exercise I got at pompom squad practice. Things started to become very festive after Thanksgiving, but I wasn't feeling it at all.

Marsha and Tina came by our room on the Monday after Thanksgiving break, wearing headbands with felt reindeer antlers. I told them I didn't have time for a bunch of silly crap and asked them to leave, probably hurting their feelings. I kept saying I wanted to study, so people would leave me alone, but whenever I picked up a book I couldn't concentrate on it. I had no interest in my classwork. People all over campus were talking about the possibility of some cataclysmic computer meltdown that was supposedly going to happen when the clock ticked over to January 1, 2000. The rumor was that computer programmers had set things up for two-digit dates, such as 99, and the need for a four-digit date, such as 2000, would really screw things up. I'd heard that before, but Steve had said he thought it was bullshit.

Steve finally called me on December 1 and asked if he could drop by, and it was as if a little part of me opened up and started breathing again. I said, "Sure." I was amazed at how little pride I had and how much I wanted him to hold me.

"I brought you something," he said when he arrived. In a small wrapped gift box, I found a pair of emerald-cut peridot earrings. "I thought they would bring out the color of your eyes," he said. I thanked him, and he asked, "Well, don't I at least get a hug?" When his arms were around me, I didn't want him to let go. I thought I might fly into pieces if he did.

We were having sex when Nancy came in that night. She grabbed her things and headed for the study. Steve left before I awakened, but I was okay with that. I had finally been able to get a decent night's sleep. I smiled when I noticed that he'd left his wristwatch on my nightstand and wondered if he intentionally left things so he'd have to come back. That morning, I went to class with more spark and interest. I started thinking maybe I could pull through and do okay for the semester.

Steve came back for his wristwatch after dinner and made love to me. Yes, I mean made love to me. He was so gentle and attentive. I felt like a princess. That week, we settled into a routine together of meeting for study time in the afternoon to get ready for final exams. Then we'd have dinner together. Then we'd study some more, and then we'd make love and sleep curled up in each other's arms. That lasted until December 13, the first day of final exams. That night I asked if he'd like to visit me sometime over Christmas break, and he said, "We're not engaged, you know."

I felt as if I'd been slapped. "What brought that on?"

He rolled onto his back and said, "You've been getting very clingy lately."

I looked at him hard and said, "And you *haven't*? What the hell is wrong with you?"

He started picking up his things and said, "I'm going back to my room. I need some space."

"Fine." And I felt it was fine for about five minutes, and then everything started to crumble inside of me.

When Nancy came in, I was crying softly in my bed. "I don't have to ask what's wrong," she said. "I wish you were more like me." I turned my back to her and tried to go to sleep, but I was on that wild, emotional roller-coaster ride again, and sleep wouldn't come. What's worse, I had an eight o'clock final in political science the next day. After Nancy went to sleep, I got up and went down the hall to see who was still up. I found Tina in the parlor and asked if she had anything that would help me sleep. I followed her to her room, where she gave me a Vicodin pill left over from when she had her wisdom teeth removed. "Do you also have something that will wake me up for my exam at eight?" I asked.

"I'll call you at seven fifteen," she said. "You can have one of the Dexedrine pills I take for ADHD."

I managed to get through exam week. Fortunately, I only had one early morning exam. I wanted to call Steve, but I was afraid he'd never come back if I appeared too needy. Instead, I called his roommate, George, when I knew Steve was taking a math exam. I think it was George's encouragement more than anything else that helped me hang on. George agreed to come over and talk to me. "But it'll cost you," he said.

"Cost me what?"

"I want beanie weenies and potato chips."

"No problem."

We sat on the floor, ate, and tried to figure Steve out. "I have no idea what's up with him," George said. Still, he insisted that Steve was very attached to me.

I crunched on a potato chip and asked, "How do you know?"

"Because he doesn't talk about you the same way he talks about other girls. You should have heard the insulting stuff he said about that bimbo at the Dragon's Den. He looked at her as one notch above a whore. He doesn't talk about you at all. I can also tell by the way that he looks at you. I think you've really gotten to him, and it must scare him. I mean, he's not in a position to be tied down, with his plans for med school and all."

Chapter 13

A Bit of Christmas Magic

Nancy insisted that I go with her and Jane to shop for the women and kids in the shelter. Gamma Nu had raised $1739 from the popcorn sales and member contributions to the cause. That was about $108 per person. We went to a toy store first, armed with wish lists from the shelter kids. A heavyset man with a white mustache approached and asked if he could help us find anything. His nametag identified him as Norman Booth, Store Manager, so I decided to tell him about our project. "Mind if I see your lists?" he asked, so we handed them over. After glancing over the lists, he asked, "How much do you want to spend on each child?" When we told him, he pulled out a calculator and started working numbers. Then he turned back to us and said, "We sell kids' clothing too, you know. If you can get the shelter to give me a receipt for tax purposes, I'll give you a sweater and a pair of jeans for each of those ten kids if you'll buy a one-hundred-dollar gift card for each of them from this store. Then you'll have the outfits, and the leftover eight dollars per child would add an extra $13.33 to each of the six mothers' gifts. How about that?"

We jumped on the idea, of course, delighted. He let Nancy use his office phone to call the shelter's director and make sure the tax receipt would not be a problem. Once that was confirmed, he helped us find the right sizes in a selection of designer brands. The manager threw in complimentary deluxe gift wrapping, which included snowman paper with big red bows and a snowman plush toy tied to each package. We thanked him, and I asked for his business card so we could send him a thank-you note.

"Wow, that was like something that would happen in a movie," Jane said as we walked to the car. We put the boxes in the trunk and debated over where to go for the women's gifts.

"We could try to make something similar happen with their gifts," I said. "Let's try a major department store." Mr. Booth's generosity had lifted my mood, and I was ready for some more Christmas magic.

It took us three tries, but we found another store manager who was willing to help with our project. Margaret Stevens offered to give us beautiful pastel cardigan and shell sweater sets in a soft angora blend if we bought six gift cards for the women with our remaining money. The sweaters sets retailed for sixty dollars. "If we do that, will you provide gift wrapping?" Nancy asked. I knew we were going to do it regardless, and Ms. Stevens probably knew that, too, but she said, "Sure." She used red foil paper with green bows.

"Can you believe what we've got here, all in less than three hours?" Jane asked when we left the store with the packages. The store managers had added over nine hundred dollars' worth of gifts to what we were able to buy.

"Ho! ho! ho! Let's go deliver this stuff," I said, so we took off for the shelter, following directions the director had given us. We'd had to sign papers saying that we wouldn't disclose the actual location of the shelter to others. This was to protect the safety of the women.

Later that night, Steve came by and apologized for his behavior. Unfortunately, Nancy was in the study with me, and she heard him and got into the conversation. "You ought to be sorry," she said. "If she were smart, she'd tell you to—"

"Hey!" I said, "We don't need your input."

"Well, you're going to get it as a free bonus. If you'd quit pining over him and go out with other guys, you'd be a lot better off!"

I looked over at her, surprised that she'd raised her voice. She hadn't done that before.

"So you're saying I should sleep with anybody and everybody, just like you?" I said. "You're lucky you don't have a disease!"

Nancy scowled and said, "Go to hell!" She left, slamming the door behind her.

Steve stood there a moment, looking at the door, and then he said, "I brought you something." He reached into his backpack and pulled out a box wrapped in green paper and tied with metallic gold string. I opened it and found a wooden box that played music. It was about the right size for storing cards or letters. It played a portion of Madonna's "Crazy for You." It seemed to me the song title had double meaning for both of us. I figured that if I could be a little crazy, I could allow Steve to be a little crazy too, as long as he was crazy for me.

"I don't have a gift for you," I said.

"Will you write me a coupon for a back rub?" he asked. I smiled, picked up a pen, and wrote, "The coupon is good for one back rub, redeemable upon request" on a scrap of paper.

"Okay, here's your gift."

He grinned and said, "I'd like to redeem it now." Naturally, his back rub turned into quite a bit more. Later, we decided to go back to his room that night to give Nancy time to cool off. "Do you think I should leave her a note of apology?" I asked.

He shrugged and said, "Did you say something that wasn't true?" I skipped writing Nancy a note.

Steve's roommate, George, had already left campus, so we had the room to ourselves and settled into a night of lovemaking and cuddling. I loved waking up to him and feeling his warm skin against mine. Just before I left to go back to my dorm, Steve announced that his family was going on a skiing trip during the holidays, so he probably wouldn't get a chance to talk to me until January. On my way back to my room, I wondered if that was just an excuse, but I had no way of knowing. I just knew I had to be back in my room by 10:00 a.m., because Dad was coming to take me home for Christmas Break.

Nancy was there when I walked in, but she didn't say anything. It became obvious that there was a big white elephant in the room, and I knew I'd have to apologize to make it go away. "Look, I'm sorry about what I said last night. I didn't mean it."

"Yes, you did."

"Okay, I did, but not in a mean way. I just think you should be careful. I care what happens to you."

"That's the same reason I said something about your relationship with Steve. Can't you see what he's doing to you?"

I twisted a strand of hair around my fingers like a little girl, caught myself, and dropped my hands to my sides. "I don't think he means to, and I'm not sure he can help it."

"But you *can* help it. When someone tries to take you on a nasty emotional trip, you don't have to go. I just think you should date some other guys."

I said, "I'll think about it," just to make her shut up.

Dad seemed a little edgy on the way home, so I finally asked if anything was wrong. "No," he said, "but I have another surprise, and I'm not sure how you'll feel about it." He looked over at me, so I lifted an eyebrow. "Carol and I got married last week at the Justice of the Peace's office downtown. She's already moved some of her furniture in and changed things around."

I told Dad I could handle that, but I almost felt as if I'd walked into another house when he opened the front door. Our boring old house with the cream-colored walls had been transformed into an explosion of color. The living room was now red with gold-and-royal-blue striped drapes. A Christmas tree stood in one corner, bare except for strands of lights, filling the room with its scent. I know they'd held off decorating it so I could take part in hanging the ornaments. The dining room was gold, with forest-green drapes and swags. Carol had taken our old dining room set and antiqued it so that it was mostly green, with areas of brown where she'd "distressed" it. All of this sounds ugly, but it wasn't ugly. It looked as if an interior decorator had come in. Familiar pictures, vases, lamps, and trinkets had been replaced with things that looked like they belonged in rooms with these colors. I went to look at the kitchen and saw that Carol hadn't gotten to it yet. Even though the effect was pleasing to the eye, it was a little hard on my mind to grasp that someone had redone "my" home without consulting me.

I walked around, speechless, until Carol came in and said, "Like it?"

"How did you do all this so fast?" I asked.

"We both took some vacation time," Dad explained.

"Where's our old stuff?"

"Your father wanted to donate it to Goodwill, but I told him we should let you go through it first to see if there are things you'd like to keep. It's all in the basement." I nearly cried when she said that. I really loved Carol for not tossing that stuff out.

"This is really different from what you did in my room," I said.

Carol nodded and said, "These are colors I love. We did your room in colors you like best." I felt blessed to have Carol as part of the family.

On December 21, my grade report arrived, and I was very disappointed to see that my grade-point average had dropped to 3.50. I didn't have the heart to tell Dad. I just decided to work harder next semester. I wondered if Steve still had his 4.0 average. I figured he probably did. *If he saw my grade report, he'd probably dump me because he'd think I was a moron,* I thought. Something about seeing my grade report made me think of Nancy's warnings about my relationship with Steve. It wasn't healthy, she'd claimed. It obviously wasn't good for my academic standing, either. To make sure the grade report wouldn't end up in Dad's hands, I burned it in our fireplace.

On Christmas Eve, I went shopping with Carol. Our family didn't usually do a lot of gifts, so I wasn't expecting much, maybe a sweater or something from him and Carol. I was debating over whether to get them individual gifts or one larger gift for both of them. As Carol backed her Ford Taurus out of the driveway, I asked if she knew of anything Dad needed or wanted that I could get for around thirty bucks. She said she thought he could use a new pair of jeans. "What about you?"

"Oh, I don't need anything. You should save your money for school." It was fun to go out and mostly just look at stuff with Carol. I bought a pair of jeans for my dad, as she'd suggested. While Carol went to look at a Holly Farms display, I purchased a scarf for her in tones of red, royal blue, and gold. It seemed just right. I saw a pair of pink slippers made like flip-flops and wondered if David and Deanna were still honeymooning in sunny Florida. I hoped not. I hoped they'd come home to a cold, hard reality. Then I felt guilty for thinking that way.

At least I had Steve, who was "crazy" for me. The only problem was that his kind of crazy wasn't always a good thing.

Later that day, Carol, Dad, and I hung the ornaments on our Christmas tree, a combination of old ones that Dad and I had kept and some that had belonged to Carol. I couldn't help but feel a twinge of sorrow that my mom wasn't the woman of the house, but even so, I was starting to like Carol more and more. We tucked our gifts under the tree, and there were six packages in all. We had each purchased one gift for the others.

On Christmas morning, I awakened to the smell of coffee and French toast. Carol had also sliced apples, oranges, and kiwi fruit and arranged it on a platter. When I came downstairs, she asked if it would be okay with me if she used my mother's Christmas dishes. I appreciated having her ask, even though she didn't have to ask my permission. I got the dishes out of the china cabinet and set the table for her. After we ate, we headed to the living room to open presents. Dad said he'd like me to open my present from Carol first, so I did. She'd found a very nice makeup kit with twenty-four shades of eye shadow, six lipsticks, six blushes, six eye pencils, and a mascara. It was all packaged neatly in a box shaped like a small train case. "Thank you—this is just awesome!" I said, and I meant it.

I had them open their gifts from me, and Carol really seemed to love the scarf I'd chosen for her. It happened to go well with the blue sweater she was wearing, so she draped in across her shoulders and tied it in an elegant knot on her left. I made a mental note to get her to show me how to do that sometime. I could tie a knot, but not an elegant-looking knot. Dad also liked his jeans and said he'd needed another pair. I watched while Carol and Dad opened their gifts from each other: a watch for Carol and a new electric razor for Dad. Then Dad placed his gift for me in my hands, a medium-sized box wrapped with blue paper and metallic silver ribbons. I opened the box and found two smaller packages inside, both wrapped in the same blue paper with silver ribbons. One was slightly larger than the other. "Open the bigger one first," Dad said.

Excited, I opened it and found a beautiful pair of diamond stud earrings.

"They're from your mother's engagement ring," he said.

I hugged him and said, "Thank you, Daddy."

"Now open the other one."

With trembling fingers, I opened the second package. Inside, I found my mother's wedding band, with the small pave-set diamonds gleaming beautifully. He'd had it refurbished for me. My tears started flowing. I couldn't help it.

On Christmas night, my dad asked about my plans after graduation. I told him I hadn't given it much thought. "I've been too busy," I said, knowing that wasn't the truth. It just sounded better than saying I'd been on too much of an emotional upheaval to care. Dad pointed out that it was time to start sending applications to four-year colleges and applying for scholarships, so I promised to go to the financial-aid office at Fermen, to get some information on scholarships, and to start sending out applications.

"Have you thought about where you'd like to transfer?" Dad asked.

I hadn't, but I said, "Maybe to Washington and Lee." I could see myself following Steve wherever he went, and I doubted he'd be rejected when he applied to the premed program at Washington and Lee.

"Nice choice, but you know you'll have to get scholarship money to do that." I nodded. Dad patted my shoulder and said, "I can't wait to see what you make of yourself." I went up to my room, thinking about Steve. I hoped he was having a good time on his ski trip. I decided to spend the rest of Christmas break, starting on Monday, December 27, researching scholarships and mailing out requests for college application packets.

Chapter 14

A New Millennium

The New Year came without the predicted computer catastrophes. I watched the ball drop in Times Square from the comfort of our living room. I'd gotten used to the red walls and other explosive colors. Watching people kiss on TV made me wish I were with Steve. Then I wondered whether his ski-trip story had been a lie. I wondered if he was kissing some other girl right at that moment. Then I let my thoughts flit to David and his new bride. That sort of thinking made for a sucky start to the New Year. I made a resolution not to let myself become anxious and edgy if Steve turned cold toward me again.

Dad drove me back to Fermen on Sunday, January 2, so I could be up and ready for classes on Monday. I walked over to have dinner in the cafeteria that evening and stopped to look at an announcement board in the lobby. The notice that caught my eye was printed on hot-pink paper: "Fermen's Y2K Campus Sweetheart Competition will be held on February 12. Entry deadline is January 10. Entry fee is $25. The competition will consist of personal interview, talent, evening gown, and one onstage interview question.

Winner will receive a crown, trophy, satin sash, flowers, and $500 and will reign as Fermen's Campus Sweetheart at the annual Valentine's Day Dance. Most Beautiful Dress, Miss Congeniality, and Interview Award will also be selected, with plaques given in these categories. Regulations in student handbook also apply as rules. Entrants must be able to attend meetings and rehearsals on Monday nights from 7:00-9:00 p.m. from January 17 through February 7. Applications available at the information desk in Stanton Hall." I sensed someone looking over my shoulder, and I turned. "You should enter," said Wanda.

"Me? I don't think I'd have a chance. Are you going to enter?"

"I've checked, and I'm not qualified," she said. "I'm on academic probation."

"Then how did you get to be prom queen?" I asked.

"I didn't ask or enter anything to become prom queen. That was by popular vote." She started to take out a cigarette but put it back, probably because she remembered she was in a building where smoking wasn't allowed. "If you enter, let me know. I'd be glad to do your face up for you like I did at the homecoming dance." She walked away from me suddenly, and I hung back for a minute, staring at the announcement. I wondered if there was any chance I could win.

Steve dropped by that evening, and we had the room to ourselves for a while, because Nancy wasn't back on campus yet. When I told him about the Campus Sweetheart competition, he encouraged me to enter. "Wanda said I should enter and even offered to do my makeup."

"Go for it." He then told me about the ski trip in such vivid detail that I was sure he'd actually taken the trip. It felt good to know he hadn't lied about it to avoid me over the holidays. We had sex while listening to an old Louis Armstrong recording he'd brought with him. By the time Nancy came in, he was up and dressed, ready to head back to his dorm. I wanted him to stay or take me with him, but I was afraid to suggest it. I didn't want him to stop being "crazy" for me. I should have known the good times wouldn't last.

After a week, I had adjusted to a new class schedule. Pompom squad and my duties at Gamma Nu were keeping me busy, too. Now that the Christmas project was completed, we started focusing on making life hellish for our pledges. Eight new girls were hoping to become permanent members, but they'd have to jump through the hoops we devised for them and make it through the "tabernacle of truth" first. Of course, we still sold popcorn on movie night, so we had to find a good way to use that money. I made a motion that we donate it to the Big Brothers Big Sisters organization, and the motion carried. I wondered what had become of Katya, the "little sister" I'd worked with last year before Wanda had nearly ruined my life. I hoped all was well with Katya.

On January 10, I remembered the deadline for the Campus Sweetheart competition and decided to enter, so I took my checkbook and headed to Stanton Hall to fill out an application. I saw the entry form would take a while to complete because, in addition to giving my name, student ID number, campus address, and phone number, I also had to write a one-page essay explaining why I felt I should be the next campus sweetheart. I was about to just forget the whole thing, but the woman behind the information counter must have noticed my dazed expression, because she told me I could just drop off the check and the first page of the application and then bring my essay to the first meeting. I paid the fee and hurried from Stanton Hall to the gymnasium for pompom squad practice.

After we'd finished rehearsing our routine, I told Wanda that I'd entered, and then I went off to find Nancy, Tina, and Marsha and tell them. I wondered if Steve would think more of me I if won. Tina seemed very excited for me, judging by the rapidity of her hand motions as she congratulated me and suggested possible dance moves I could use in the talent competition. Marsha and Nancy were more subdued. They sat on Nancy's bed and listened to us make plans.

In the cafeteria the next day, I headed over to where Steve and George were sitting and plopped my breakfast tray on the table. I was eager to tell them I'd entered the Campus Sweetheart competition. I left briefly to get a glass of milk, and George was leaving when I came back. "Time to head out to math class," he said, tipping me a nod.

Steve was rather quiet, which seemed unusual to me. "Everything okay?" I asked.

He didn't answer for a moment, but then he looked at me and said, "I think we need to spend some time apart."

"But we just spent Christmas break apart," I said. I realized my voice had a shrill edge to it, and that reminded me of Deanna, who was now David's wife. I didn't want to sound that way. A wild, unsettled feeling began to stir in me, and I was afraid to say anything else.

"I guess that wasn't long enough," he said.

It was snowing, and classes were cancelled the following day, so Nancy and I both slept in. I got up around 11:00

a.m., headed over to the cafeteria for an early lunch, and ran into George. I told him about entering the Campus Sweetheart competition, and he said he'd be rooting for me. Then I told him what Steve had said at breakfast the day before. "You're kidding," he said. "I don't know what's wrong with him." With a mischievous look on his face, George stepped into the quad and started forming a snowball.

"Don't you dare throw that—" *Whomp!* The snowball landed on my shoulder, and that meant war. I chased him into the open area in front of Baylor Hall and nailed him in the chest with a big snowball.

I realized then that he had made a small arsenal in advance of the fight, because he started pulling snowball from his pockets and hurling them my way. "Wait, that's not fair!" *Whomp! Whomp-whomp!*

I picked what was left of one and said, "I'm going to make you eat this!" And the game was on. I chased him until he slowed and let me tackle him, and then I tried to pry his lips apart to insert the snow. Then I started tickling him, and George finally parted his lips, but instead of taking the snow, he pushed my hands down and kissed my lips. "I think Steve is an idiot," he whispered.

On the afternoon of January 17, I sat staring at a blank sheet of paper. A one-page essay wasn't much, but I couldn't put anything together that sounded right about why I wanted to be the next campus sweetheart. Some answers came to mind, but I didn't think the judges would be impressed: *Because I'm a pathetic loser who can't hold on to a boyfriend. Because I have serious mental problems and will wish I'm dead if I don't win. Because I need a little respect.*

When Nancy came in thirty minutes later, the page was still blank. "Help me, Nancy. Why am I doing this?"

Chapter 15

A New Campus Sweetheart

The assembly room in Stanton Hall was packed on January 17 at 7:00 p.m. At this first meeting for the Campus Sweetheart competition, I learned that seventy-five girls had entered. We had two weeks to put together a three-minute talent routine for the competition, which we would perform for a panel of judges on January 31 or February 1, depending on which time slot we picked. Being late was grounds for disqualification. The judges would select the top fifteen from the talent competition, and these would continue in the competition. The rest would be out. The fifteen finalists would then have a week to get ready for the personal interview portion. Whoever became the next campus sweetheart would get to perform her talent routine at the Valentine's Day dance.

Danna had entered, and so had Jane, Tammy, and Hillary. I knew the talent competition would be stiff for those who chose to do dance routines. What was worse, we would all have to wait in the lobby to be called into the auditorium to perform for the judges. We wouldn't get a chance to see what type of routines the other girls were doing unless we saw them practicing somewhere on campus before the judging began. I turned in my essay and left the meeting feeling less than optimistic regarding my chances. I also knew I'd have to wear the dress I'd worn to the Homecoming Dance for the evening gown competition. I doubted a seventy-nine-dollar dress from J.C. Penney would earn the Most Beautiful Dress award. The whole thing was going to be a wash for me, as I saw it. I was too high-strung and irritable to become Miss Congeniality, and I'd probably blow my personal interview by admitting to the judges that the things I'd written on my essay were pure bullshit. *This is such a total waste of time,* I thought as I looked over the sign-up sheet for time slots. I chose the very last one on Tuesday, February 1. *That way, my performance will still be fresh in their minds when they pick the finalists,* I thought. On top of that, I was depressed because Steve hadn't called me. I decided to drop by his room to get his take on the situation and see if his mood had changed.

Wanda saw me in the quad and asked about the competition. When I told her I thought the talent competition would be stiff, she said, "Not necessarily."

"What do you mean?"

"Dean Asher is on the judging panel. He's a lecher. Just do a super-sexy routine, and you'll win his vote." I looked at her and could tell she was absolutely serious. "Have you got some time? I've got a lot of music, including Broadway musicals, in my room. I could help you work something up tonight."

I looked at my watch. "Well, I was going to go over to Steve's room, but I guess we could look at some stuff."

When we got to her room, Wanda headed straight for the CD of the Broadway musical *All that Jazz*. "What kind of dance outfits do you have?" she asked.

"Nothing but my pompom squad outfit and my regular clothes."

Wanda just shook her head. She opened a drawer and looked through her things, while I looked around her room. The room looked stark, because she had decorated everything in black and white, and there were no pictures or posters on the walls. She pulled out a pair of black tights, a short black skirt, and a black midriff-length top. "Here, go try these on," she said, pointing me toward the bathroom. I came out in the skimpy outfit, feeling a little shy. She started the soundtrack, tossed me a black fedora, and said, "Show me some sass."

I fell into character and started kicking and strutting around to the music. "Cover your tummy with that hat and then drop it down to your side," she suggested. We added her desk chair as a prop, because she remembered that from seeing the play, and we worked out some moves. "I know a guy who can edit this track down to exactly three minutes," she told me when we had put a routine together. "Come back tomorrow and we'll tweak routine. This will beat anything that involves shaking pompoms. Just wait and see."

The next night, I went back to Wanda's room. She had me put the black outfit on again, and this time she did my makeup before we started working on the dance moves. That really helped me get into character and vamp out. "Why are you doing this?" I asked.

"I wanted to do something to help make up for what I did last year. Also, I'd wanted to enter and work up a routine. If I help you, I can take part in the competition vicariously. Fair enough?"

"Fair enough." We kept working for another half an hour. "I want to try this out on Steve," I said when we were done.

"Don't have sex with him afterwards if you do," she said. "That'll make him crazy." When I was leaving, she told me to take the outfit with me so I could practice in it every day. "Just wash it in cold water, and let it drip dry." I left her room, wearing the outfit under my winter coat, and hurried over to Steve's dorm.

Steve wasn't in, but George was there, so I put the CD on and showed him the routine we'd worked up. "You're gonna win it," he said. "Can I walk you back to your dorm?"

"Sure. Bring your books, and we'll make it a study date. I have a calculus test tomorrow."

Back at my dorm, I changed into some jeans and a sweater before we hit the books. George had brought over a stack of library books and a packet of index cards and started research for a history paper. Sometimes I'd look over at him and catch him looking at me, and we'd both look away quickly, and then we'd glance back at one another and smile. I liked George's easy manner.

The next day I aced my calculus test. I didn't get the grade that day, but I just knew it. I was glad George had studied by my side. At pompom squad practice, I heard that Tammy and Hillary were planning to do routines with their pompoms in the talent competition. I watched them performing perfect splits and jumps and wondered if my dance routine had a chance against theirs. Wanda must have sensed my concern, because she came over afterward and said, "Don't worry about topping their routines. I've seen them, and they're pretty good, but not as good as yours."

Steve was waiting outside the gymnasium for me, which was a very nice surprise. "George says you've got a killer talent routine lined up for the Campus Sweetheart competition," he said.

"I think it will work." We walked across the grass toward my dorm while I wondered if Steve was ready to spend time with me again. Even as I thought about that, I knew I shouldn't have to wonder such things about a boyfriend.

He put his arm around me and pulled me closer to him. "I've behaved badly, and that isn't fair to you. I guess I'm just scared of commitment. When I start to feel for you, I just want to shut down sometimes. I'm going to stop it. You deserve better than that." It wasn't exactly an apology, but his words made my spirits soar. I wanted so much to be with him and to be happy. "Can we study together tonight?" he asked. I smiled and took his hand. *Yes, and we can do a lot more than that,* I thought. It turned out that we never studied that night, because we were all over each other after I showed him my dance routine.

At 3:00 p.m. on February 1, I dressed and made my way over to Stanton Hall for the talent competition. Wanda was waiting for me in a dressing room backstage, as she had promised. In true Broadway style, the dressing-room mirror had light bulbs all around it. I watched as Wanda did my makeup with a very heavy hand. "Do you want me to look like a real whore?" I asked.

"No, those stage lights will wash you out if I don't do this. Believe me; your makeup will look normal from the judges' seats." She pinned my hair into a messy updo and massaged my shoulders a bit before sending me out to wait for them to call me from the lobby. I noticed that when they called for someone who wasn't there, they immediately called the next name. A girl named Rita Meadows missed her call while I was waiting, and I wondered what had made her late. That meant instant disqualification, according to the rules. When they called for me, I felt calm. I walked up the side stairs onto the empty stage, where Wanda had placed a single straight-back wooden chair for me to use as a prop. I had the black fedora in my hand. I could smell the dusty stage curtains as they closed in front of me. Then the curtains opened and my music started. I kicked, strutted, and ground my hips throughout my three-minute shot at making the finalists. My routine worked well, and I tried to put some extra sass into it, since my winning would be Wanda's vicarious win. I almost felt like I was seducing that chair. At the end, we had planned for me to sit in the chair and wave the hat overhead, but on a whim, I went into a full split with my right leg in front of me and my left leg behind me, waved the hat at the judges, and winked. Afterward I demonstrated the modified ending for Wanda. "You've made the finals," she said.

"How do you know?"

"I just do."

The next day I received notice that I'd been selected as one of the fifteen finalists. Nancy and I danced around our room, and then Tina and Marsha came in and joined the celebration. Tina threw her arms out in a wide arc and said, "You can win the whole thing now!"

I stopped celebrating suddenly, because at that moment, I felt like Cinderella in a peasant dress. "I need a better evening gown," I said.

"Then we'll find you one," Nancy said. "Let's see what Tina's blue dress is like on you."

I tried it, but it was way too long. We spent a long time going up and down the hall, borrowing dresses for me to try on. Wanda came into the parlor while a group of girls hovered around me trying to see if we could pin Clarissa's stunning red evening gown to fit better around my bust. I was wearing a pushup bra, but it didn't help enough. "Ladies," she said, "you're going about this wrong. You need to make her bust fit the gown! Just hang on. I'll be right back." Within minutes, she was back with two rubbery-looking falsies. "Here, stick these under your breasts." I did, and then I not only filled out the dress, but I appeared to have very nice cleavage.

"Are you sure it's okay if I wear it?"

"Of course it's okay. I want a Gamma Nu girl to win."

I promised to have her dress dry-cleaned after the competition.

My dad called that evening, and I told him about the Campus Sweetheart competition. "Maybe I should come up," he said.

"No, that's okay. It's not that big of a deal. I don't think anyone else's parents are coming." I wasn't sure about that, but I felt awkward about having Dad come and hang around afterward. It seemed those moments should belong to Steve and me.

Steve and I had settled back into seeing each other every day, so I felt like I was glowing from the inside out most of the time. Nancy and Rob were seeing each other a lot, as well. I liked that, because I wasn't coming in to find her in bed with "mystery men" anymore. Usually, she stayed in Rob's room if they spent a whole night together.

Steve and I slept together some nights, but we also managed to get a lot of studying done. One night George came by and asked if he could study with me, but he saw Steve was already there. He gave me a wistful look and said, "Maybe another time."

On the day before the Campus Sweetheart competition, Steve had promised to come over, escort me to Stanton Hall on my big night, and cheer me on. The competition started at 7:00 p.m., but I needed to be there by six at the latest. At five o'clock, I hadn't heard from Steve, and I started feeling anxious. I called Steve's room, and George answered and told me he hadn't seen Steve since early that morning. "Don't panic," he said. "I'll find him for you."

At five-thirty, George knocked on my door. "Don't worry," he said. "He'll eventually turn up." I left him a note saying that I'd save him a seat near the front if he got there after the competition had begun. George carried the dress bag and another bag I'd packed with things I needed, and he walked with me over to Stanton Hall. I smiled and thanked George for helping me. "Knock 'em dead," he said. I smiled and nodded, but I was trembling on the inside.

Wanda was waiting for me in the dressing room, which had a long mirror, surrounded by lights, over a counter that ran the length of the room. There were little velvet-cushioned metal chairs at various stations along the mirror. She handed me the schedule, which had been secret until tonight, and I saw I would be the fourth girl to go on in the talent portion. "Are you ready?" she asked, and two tears rolled down my cheeks.

When I told her what was wrong, she let out a stream of profanity that would burn most people's ears. She took me by the shoulders and said, "You need to pretend that he's here and everything is right in your world. If you can't put the emotions on hold, you're done. Freak after the competition, not now. Do you understand me?"

I nodded and wiped my eyes. Wanda said, "It's a good thing they have the evening gown part before the talent part, or we'd have to totally redo your face, and we probably wouldn't have time for that, since you go on fourth." I sat down and let Wanda brush my hair and curl it with a curling iron. She did my makeup with a lighter hand than she planned to use for the talent competition, and I stepped into Clarissa's dress. The red velvet sheath fit like a glove, with the help of Wanda's falsies. It flared out at the bottom in a fan of red netting material. Wanda used a red-sequined comb to pull my hair back from my face on one side. I wore the diamond earrings Dad had given me for Christmas. I was ready when they called for us to line up in alphabetical order. When our names were called, we were to enter from stage right, walk to center stage, turn slowly around so the judges could see our dresses from every angle, wave to the crowd, and exit at stage left.

When it was my turn, I started searching the front rows of the crowd as I walked. I reached center stage, turned and waved, and then I saw George in the second row with an empty seat beside him. Steve had missed one of my big moments. I felt my heart sink but tried to keep my nose to the sky, as Daddy would have said, as I walked off the stage.

Our personal interviews had taken place the day before, and mine had seemed to go well. The judges had asked about my academics, and I'd told them about receiving a full scholarship. When they asked about my future goals, I told them I'd applied to Washington and Lee, and that I hoped to major in political science. They seemed to be impressed with those details, along with the fact that I was a coleader of the pompom squad and vice president of Gamma Nu.

It seemed like no time before the emcee said, "Now that you've seen the girls, we're going to give you a chance to get to know them a little better. In a moment, each girl will come out and give a one-minute answer to a question, based on the information given in her personal interview. I was fifteenth in the line-up for that portion of the competition. I figured that surely Steve would be there by then.

He wasn't. I stepped out to center stage and saw his empty seat. I heard the emcee say, "And now we'll hear from Samantha Fredrich." I started looking toward the back and sides of the auditorium, thinking Steve must surely be somewhere on the fringes of the crowd, but I couldn't find him. Then I realized the emcee was waiting for me to respond. I hadn't even heard the entire question he had asked me, but it included something about a role model. I knew it would be the kiss of death to ask him to repeat the question, so I said, "As the judges know, I'm very interested in serving as a role model for younger girls. Last year, I served as a Big Sister and worked with a young girl named Katya. It was so gratifying to see her gradually start to come out of her shell." I suddenly realized I had no idea where I was going with this, so I said, "That's why I plan to pursue a degree in political science. I've applied to Washington and Lee University . . . Thank you." I smiled, waved, and exited stage left.

There was applause, but not the thunderous applause that had followed some of the other girls' responses. Backstage, a girl I didn't know looked at me and asked, "What the hell were you mumbling about out there?" I kept my eyes to the floor and kept walking. By the time it was my turn in the talent competition, I was very nervous and unsettled.

My dance routine went very well because I had rehearsed so much, and I suppose I was trying hard, hoping Steve was out there somewhere in the audience. I wanted him to be proud of me. During parts of it, I was aware of George supporting me as best he could. When I did my split and winked at the end, he was on his feet, whistling with his fingers in his mouth. The seat beside him was still empty.

When everyone had performed, the emcee had us all come out for one last walk across the stage and a chance to wave at the crowd while the judges tallied the scores. This time, instead of exiting stage left, we went to stand in a line of spaces marked with masking tape to keep us the right distance apart. "And now, the results are in," the emcee said. "The first award, for Most Beautiful Dress goes to . . ." he said, and there was a pause while he opened an envelope, "Miss Jennifer Anne Knollwood!" He presented a plaque to a buxom brunette, who had worn a low-cut, black-sequined gown. Miss Congeniality went to Danna, and I was glad for her. The Interview Award went to Hillary. "And now," the emcee said, "we'll learn who will be our next Campus Sweetheart." There was a drum roll, and he opened the envelope and read, "Miss Tammy Lynn Sanders!" We all gathered around Tammy and exchanged hugs with her after she'd received her sash and crown and a bouquet of red roses. I was truly happy for Tammy, and then a dreadful thought crossed my mind: *What if Steve had known I had no chance and had stayed away to avoid being embarrassed by escorting a loser?* Steve had let me down many times since I'd met him. I was hurt, of course, but I also felt bitter toward him. *Why did he have to let me down tonight, of all nights? And why am I letting it rattle me so?* Then I remembered again what my mother had said to me on her deathbed: "Don't let bitterness poison your life." I wanted to tell her that sometimes it was a little hard not to do that. Then I thought of what George had done to try to calm me and make up for Steve's absence, and I felt a rush of tenderness toward him. I hugged Wanda and thanked her for all she'd done before I left. "Sorry I didn't win," I said.

"That's okay. I just wanted to be part of this, and I think you did great."

George met me outside the dressing room a few minutes later. "You did great!" he said. "I'm really proud of you."

"I lost."

He took my hand. "No, don't ever say that. There wasn't a loser in the bunch tonight, and if there'd been a talent award, they wouldn't have had any choice but to give it to you."

"Thanks, George; it's nice of you to say that."

"No, I mean it."

George walked me back to the dorm, where we found Steve waiting in my room. "Steve, what happened, man?" George asked.

"Nothing happened. I decided not to go, so she'd see she could do this on her own." He looked at me as if to make sure I'd gotten the point.

I'd gotten it all right! I couldn't believe I'd allowed him to put me through such a stinking emotional mess, not just this evening, but for weeks. Steve had been inconsiderate before, even rude, but this time something snapped inside of me. I'd had enough. "Get out of my room, Steve."

He gave me an incredulous look and said, "I'll call you when you cool off."

"Don't bother. We're through." I met his gaze calmly, because I meant it.

"Okay, I'll remind you of that next time you come begging me to hold you."

After he'd gone, George, who had been standing off to the side, asked, "Does this mean I have my study partner back?"

"It sure does."

He gave me a brilliant smile and said, "Let's go celebrate. I'll take you to anywhere you like."

"Sorry, George, I'm kind of bummed out. Could we just stay here and eat canned ravioli?"

George's big smile returned. "No problem." He sighed and added, "I'm so relieved. I thought you were about to ask me to leave, too."

Chapter 16

My Funny Valentine

I skipped the Valentine's Dance after I heard Steve had been calling down the list of other girls on the pompom squad and inviting them to go with him. I wondered what he was trying to prove, but I wasn't about to let bitterness poison my life. I decided to spend Valentine's Day studying, from the time my classes let out until I went to bed. Around 4:00 p.m., I'd just settled down with my calculus book when I heard someone knocking on our door. Clarissa had come to let me know I had visitors in the parlor downstairs, so I combed my hair, put on a touch of lip gloss and headed downstairs, not knowing whom to expect.

"Sam!" a little girl's voice squealed. It was Katya, the child I'd worked with as a Big Sister the previous year. Her mother, Natalie Combs, stood by, smiling while Katya crashed into my thighs and hugged me.

"Katya!" I said, and I picked her up. I remembered the withdrawn little girl she had been a year ago, the child who had been unable to show affection or receive it well. "Wow, she's come a long way," I said to her mother.

"Look, I brought you something," Katya said. She handed me a big red envelope. I opened it and found a handmade card. She'd drawn a spaceship with an alien inside and pasted googly eyes on the alien. Below the picture she'd scrawled, "You're out of this world. Love, Katya."

I hugged her and said, "Thank you, Katya, I love it!"

Natalie said, "She's recently started talking about you a lot. I'm glad you were in, so she could deliver her card. She made it this morning and insisted that you must have it on Valentine's Day." Just then, George came into the parlor with a heart-shaped box of candy in his hands. He sat one of the overstuffed chairs, apparently not wanting to interrupt us, so I called him over and introduced him.

"Is he your boyfriend?" Katya asked.

"No, he's just my friend."

"Then why did he bring you chocolate?"

I looked at George and asked, "Is that for me?" He nodded, so I said, "Let's open it now. I'll bet Katya would like a piece."

Katya had two pieces of chocolate and announced she'd had enough. Then she looked at George and gravely asked, "Are you going to ask her to marry you?"

George laughed and said, "I'm not sure. Do you think I should?"

"Definitely."

Natalie laughed and told Katya it was time for them to go. George and I walked with them to their car. "I hope we can visit with you again," Natalie said before they left.

"Of course."

When they had gone, George said, "I also have this for you. I hid it under my coat so the little girl wouldn't demand to see it. I found it in an antique shop downtown." He handed me an envelope.

I opened it and found a vintage Hallmark card that appeared to be from the 1970s with its purple, hot pink, and orange color-block designs and cartoon couple on the cover. It read, "This sentimental Valentine is guaranteed to bring a lump to your throat." Inside, it read, "Directions: 1.) Wad card, 2.) Chew 26 (or 27) times, 3.) Swallow." He'd signed it, "Best, George."

We went back to the parlor, retrieved my box of candy, and took it to my room. George and I had dinner together in the cafeteria and came back to my room afterward to study. Not long after George left, Nancy came in with Rob, so I grabbed my blanket and pillow and headed for the recliner in the study.

Chapter 17

Sunshine and Lollipops

I went home for spring break and found that Carol had painted all the downstairs rooms in vibrant colors. She had also unpacked all of her things, so there were pictures of strangers on the coffee tables and hanging on the wall along the hallway. It seemed weird at first, but I had grown to like Carol so much that I really didn't mind. She gave a grand tour of her photos: "This is my cousin Joe; this is my daughter, Sarah, when she was four; this is . . ."

I interrupted to ask, "Where's Sarah now?" I'd never heard that she had a daughter.

"Sarah died of a rare form of leukemia when she was six. I think my husband always blamed me, although blaming me didn't make sense. We divorced later." Carol looked as though she might tear up. I'd never had a clue Carol had experienced such sorrow. As a kid, I'd just seen her as my highly demanding swim coach.

"I'm sorry," I said and placed a hand on her shoulder. I looked for a way to change the subject and said, "I'll bet Sarah would have loved the purple in this den. Where did you find it?"

Carol looked up as though waking from a dream and said, "Oh, this? It was just a happy accident. It's not the color I asked them to mix." She walked over to a window and said, "Sarah would be fourteen now, if she'd lived."

It was sometime during spring break that I realized I wanted George as more than a friend. I found myself thinking about Steve a lot that weekend. George and I had spent a lot of time together, but I never felt panicky when I couldn't be with him. We had studied together so much that we'd just glided through our midterm exams. George was very laid back, and he never assumed anything with me. He knew I'd slept with Steve, but he had never even attempted touch me intimately. I felt that he respected me. The more I thought about him, the more I wanted to push the relationship to another level. At the same time, I realized I'd been selfish; I'd talked to him so much about my life and my problems without learning much about his. I determined to change that.

On the first day of spring, George and I were sitting on a bench in the quad admiring an explosion of tulips in the flowerbeds. I asked, "Do you remember that snowy day in February when you bombarded me with snowballs? How come you've never kissed me again?"

He ran a hand through his hair and said, "I didn't think you were attracted to me in that way."

I pushed a strand of his black hair behind his ear and said, "I'm very attracted to you," and I leaned in and gave him a kiss.

When we went to my room after dinner that evening, I was glad to see we had it to ourselves. I took his hand, and he started kissing me gently. He moved from my lips to my ear to my neck, and then he slid his hands under my shirt. I was in ecstasy before he took any of my clothes off. Though his foreplay was gentle, his lovemaking felt urgent, but he maintained full control of himself. Only after I reached orgasm did he allow himself full release. Later he lay there kissing my face, my breasts, my tummy, and telling me I was beautiful. I kept stroking his arms, his chest, and his shoulders. I hadn't realized he was so muscular until I saw him without clothes.

We were back in the study when Nancy came in with Rob, and we decided to take a walk across campus. I asked George about his childhood, and he told me about family in Oklahoma. He said his father was a Cherokee who had eloped with his mother, a blue-eyed, brown-haired farm girl. "I remember a time when I was four, and we went to see my mother's parents. She left my dad and me in the car and went to see if we would be welcome there. Her dad answered the door, and I could tell he'd said something mean, because Mom turned away. Then her mom pushed past him, came out to the car, and told my dad, "Let me take the boy. I want my husband to look at our grandson." My dad told me to go with her, so I got out, and she carried me into the house. My grandfather cursed, but then he looked at me and started to cry. From that time on, we were all welcome in their house." I traced my fingertips along his cheek after he'd told this story. I could understand why the sight of him had melted his grandfather's heart.

When I asked about his dreams for the future, George said he'd come to Fermen on a full academic scholarship and that he hoped to attend Georgetown University later. He'd been offered a scholarship to Georgetown, but it hadn't been enough, and he hadn't been able to go. "I'm fighting to prove myself here, and I've already reapplied to Georgetown. I'm going to be a lawyer," he said.

In April, George and I arranged to take Katya to a carnival that had set up on the outskirts of Vinton. Natalie seemed to appreciate our desire to do something for her daughter, and she drove us out to the place. In the parking lot, Natalie said, "I'll meet you there at the gate in two hours. Katya, be good, and—"

"Let's go," Katya said. "I want to ride the Ferris wheel."

Natalie slipped two twenty-dollar bills into my hand. "Use this for food and special treats all around. I want all of you to have fun."

Katya's dark hair was gleaming in the sun as she took off running for the main entry the minute her mother left. George called out, "Hey, slow down, little girl! You could get hit by a car," and he ran and caught her.

Entry was free, but we had to buy tickets for the rides, and it took five tickets for most rides. We bought fifty tickets, knowing we could always get more if we needed them, and we headed for the Ferris wheel. We rode it with Katya tucked safely between us, and I pretended for a moment that she was our daughter. From the top, I could hear the sounds of the carnival drifting up: the music from the carousel, the distant sound of the roller coaster running on its track, and the screams its riders made on each descent. I felt an overflow of love for George and Katya, for my dad and Carol, and the joy of being alive.

When the Ferris wheel ride was over, we bought hotdogs and Cokes for lunch. I also bought three huge multicolored lollipops and put them in my purse for us to enjoy later. We set out to find a table under a canopy where we could eat comfortably, although the area was very crowded. Afterward, I took Katya to the restroom and reapplied sunscreen to her face. When we came out, she caught sight of the bumper cars and begged to ride them. "I'm afraid of them," I told her, because I really didn't like riding them. "Get George to ride them with you." They took off, while I waited on a bench by the Tilt-a-Whirl.

I was craning to see George and Katya when a shadow fell across me. I looked up, and there was David standing in front of me. "I'd like to talk to you for a minute," he said. Anger swelled up in me, and I was about to tell him to get lost, when he said, "Please." So I nodded and slid over to make room for him to sit down. "I just felt you deserved an explanation about what happened between us. I really love you . . . loved you," he said, "but then my old girlfriend called and told me she was pregnant. I felt I had to do the right thing. That's why I said, 'it's complicated' when you asked if I were engaged." David looked miserable as he spoke, but I wasn't exactly sympathetic.

"Why did you have her call me?" I demanded. "Couldn't you have had the decency to do that yourself?"

"I didn't have her call you. She found your name and number on a scrap of paper in my desk when she came to campus looking for me. I didn't know she had it, and I had no idea she would make that call. Later, I was devastated by the whole situation. When I found out what she'd said to you, I wanted to call you, but I wasn't thinking right, and it seemed like a bad thing to do. I thought it would be better to let you think I was an asshole. I'm sorry."

"It's okay," I said. "I'm happy now. How are things going for you?"

"Fairly well. I have a daughter now, Leah Renée, three weeks old." He took out his wallet and showed me a picture.

"She's beautiful."

He nodded and said, "You're beautiful." He kissed his fingertips, touched my cheek, and walked away. I sat there wondering what he was doing in Vinton and where his wife and daughter were. I realized I might see them at the carnival somewhere in the crowd, and I realized that would be okay, because my heart was full. I had everything I wanted.

By the time we left, Katya had ridden nearly every ride and some of them twice. George had won Teddy bears for Katya and me, and we'd sampled funnel cakes, cotton candy, and candy apples. By the time Natalie dropped us off on campus, Katya was sleeping in the backseat. I gave Natalie the lollipop I'd bought for Katya and handed her the change from the money she'd given me. "You keep it," she said. "Take George to lunch or something."

When Natalie drove off, George said, "I saw David talking to you at the carnival. Are you okay?

"I'm fine." I briefly explained what David had said to me.

He looked at me intently. "Are you sure you're not going to get sad over that?"

"Not a chance," I said, and I started a tickle fight. We tumbled around on the lawn outside of Baylor Hall, until he pinned me to the ground and said, "Hey, I think we'd better take this fight inside."

The week before final exams, I received a letter stating that I'd been accepted at Washington and Lee, but I didn't care anymore. I wanted to stay near George. Carol called to ask if there was anything in particular I'd like as a graduation gift. *Yeah, a million dollars,* I thought. I told her I couldn't think of anything.

"I have some news for you," she said. "I'm going to have a baby."

I dropped the receiver and scrambled to pick it up. "A baby? . . . Congratulations!" I started shifting some things inside my heart to make room for a tiny step-sibling. "What did Dad say?"

"He nearly fainted at first, but he's pleased." I smiled inwardly, thinking how much happiness a child could bring to Carol, especially since she'd lost Sarah. "Can I speak to Dad?"

Dad told me he'd gotten a much better job about a week before he heard the news. A new company had opened in Danville and offered him more money than he'd ever made. When we hung up, I went down the hall to tell Tina and Marsha the news.

Chapter 18

The Tabernacle of Truth

Gamma Nu's final meeting of the year was always the "tabernacle of truth" meeting, where we invited others to become permanent members. This year, eight new girls were hoping to be brought into our circle. Clarissa, Nancy, Jane, and I decided to change things up. We sent the pledges on scavenger hunts, asking for some common items and some near-impossible items: a red bandana, a vial of dragon's blood, a camel, the hammer of Thor, a blue sandal, and Nefertiti's nipple ring (of course we didn't know whether Nefertiti had ever owned a nipple ring).

We thought it would be interesting to have the girls bring bogus items into the "tabernacle of truth" and convince us they were, in fact, authentic. The girls would have to use their ingenuity to find substitutes for the odd items. We called a meeting, explained the rules, and discussed the difference between literal truth and empirical truth. We then gave them two hours to come back with the items. Only four girls—Christy, Grace, Laura, and Jill—returned before the time ran out. This wouldn't exclude the others from coming to meetings, but they'd have to try again next year to be brought into the circle.

"So, you're expecting me to believe this is the hammer of Thor," I said to Christy. "It looks like an ordinary hammer to me."

"But see this mark," she said, pointing to something like appeared to be a large handprint drawn in with a magic marker. "Thor's hand burned an image into the wood. No other hand will fit perfectly within that image."

I looked at the hammer again. "Hmmm." I passed it to Nancy and asked, "What do you think?"

"It could be from the hand of Thor," she said. "We need to examine it more carefully. Did you find the nipple ring?"

"I did." Christy pulled out a piece she'd broken off a baby's pink pacifier, and showed it to us. She had scratched what appeared to be Egyptian hieroglyphics onto its surface.

"I'll accept this as authentic," Jane said immediately, and once one of us said that, the rest were sworn to agree. "I assume you have brought us a vial of dragon's blood."

"Of course." Christy brought out a tiny perfume bottle filled with green liquid.

"What is this?" I asked.

"Well, you didn't expect it to be red, did you?" We all laughed. She put the bandana, the sandal, and a camel cigarette on the table, and we told her to wait outside while we examined the hammer.

Everyone had located a blue shoe, a red bandana, and a camel of some sort. Grace brought in a sledgehammer, a gold earring, and a tube of purple lip gloss. Laura brought in a brass gavel, a ring formed from slicing the nipple of a baby's bottle, and small vial of what appeared to be rust. Jill arrived with a meat mallet, a silver belly ring, and a small jar of blackberry jam. According to our plan, one of us balked at a single item in each girl's findings. We left them all waiting for our decisions, but we quickly agreed to accept all four as permanent members of Gamma Nu.

In the parlor, we joined the pledges and the rest of our members and gathered into a circle to light candles. "There can be no lies between sisters," Clarissa said. "No falsehoods, no deceit. We are called on to stand by our fellow sisters. The circle means unity and sisterhood. The candles mean truth. If a sister comes and blows out your candle, you will step out of the circle. Is this clear?"

The girls murmured their assent.

"We will now make it known whom we feel we can trust."

Clarissa walked over and stood in front of Christy; she then moved to Grace, Laura, and Jill, allowing each girl's candle to remain lit. "Congratulations, ladies. You are now part of the inner circle of Gamma Nu."

After the ceremony, I thought about George. He had never tried to pass off bogus emotions as the real thing. We hadn't needed to discuss the difference between literal and empirical truth. I loved him for that.

Chapter 19

Graduation Day

I took my place in the graduation processional on Sunday, May 7, 2000. The ceremony took place on the lawn in the quad, and the weather was perfect for it. The tulips had faded and been replaced with banks of purple and white petunias. I was glad it wasn't too hot, since we were wearing the black gowns. I wore a blue dress with a sweetheart neckline underneath, but Tina and Marsha, along with many other girls, had opted to wear shorts and tank tops under their gowns. We all had on black pumps, and I imagined how they'd look in their shorts if they kept the shoes on after they shed the gowns—which they wouldn't, of course.

It pleased me that George was our class valedictorian. I figured that must be galling to Steve, who had always seemed so arrogant about his academic capacity. One line in George's valedictorian speech stood out to me: "If you'll be patient and stay true to your course, you can get what you want." I'd asked if he really believed that when I'd listened to him rehearse the speech the night before. "Sure," he said. "That's how I got you, isn't it? I wanted to be with you the first day I met you."

I had worked hard enough to end up with a 3.70 GPA even after messing up in the fall semester, so I was proud to walk across the stage and receive my diploma. I peeked at it and then held its black binder in my lap as I watched my friends march across the stage. When the ceremony ended, everyone was invited to stay for a reception on the south lawn. I made my way over to Dad and Carol to let them take pictures. Then George brought his parents over and introduced them, and Carol and his mother took pictures of us together. It was hard to talk to everyone at the reception, with so many people there, but I had spoken to Tina, Marsha, Clarissa, Hillary, Jane, Tammy, Danna, and Wanda the night before. We'd all exchanged addresses and talked about our future plans.

Tina was transferring across the country to Seattle University. Hillary had been accepted at Georgia Tech. Wanda's father had opened a new business, and she was taking a year off from college to travel in Europe and scope out merchandise as a buyer for it. Nancy and Rob had announced their engagement, but knowing Nancy, I wondered whether they'd ever actually get married. Clarissa, Marsha, Jane, and Danna were like me, undecided. We had been accepted at a couple of four-year schools, but we hadn't sent our deposits to any of them yet. I was leaning away from going to Washington and Lee, simply because that's where Steve was headed. George had received a full scholarship to Georgetown, so I considered doing something that would keep us close, geographically speaking. Out of all my friends, Tammy seemed to have the most intriguing plans. She had signed up with the Peace Corps.

I watched Dad and Carol, arm in arm, as they mingled with my friends and their families. To me, Carol looked more beautiful that day than she ever had, and I thought it must be because of the happiness of having a child with my dad. George hooked an arm around me and smiled. "I love you," he said. I didn't know exactly which path I'd choose, but at that moment, my future looked very bright.